TRAGIC LINKS

OTHER BOOKS BY
CATHY BEVERIDGE

Offside (Thistledown Press, 2001)
Shadows of Disaster (Ronsdale Press, 2003)
Chaos in Halifax (Ronsdale Press, 2004)
One on One (Thistledown Press, 2005)
Stormstruck (Ronsdale Press, 2006)

Tragic
LINKS

CATHY BEVERIDGE

RONSDALE PRESS

RONSDALE PRESS
3350 West 21st Avenue, Vancouver, B.C., Canada V6S 1G7
www.ronsdalepress.com

Typesetting: Julie Cochrane, in Minion 12 pt on 16
Cover Art: Ljuba Levstek
Cover Design: Julie Cochrane
Paper: Ancient Forest Friendly "Silva" (FSC) — 100% post-consumer waste,
    totally chlorine-free and acid-free

Ronsdale Press wishes to thank the following for their support of its publishing
program: the Canada Council for the Arts, the Government of Canada through
the Book Publishing Industry Development Program (BPIDP), the British Columbia Arts Council, and the Province of British Columbia through the British
Columbia Book Publishing Tax Credit program.

Library and Archives Canada Cataloguing in Publication

Beveridge, Cathy
    Tragic links / Cathy Beveridge.

ISBN 978-1-55380-066-8

    1. Québec Bridge Disaster, Québec, 1907 — Juvenile fiction.
2. Laurier Palace Movie Theatre Fire, Montréal, Québec,
1927 — Juvenile fiction. I. Title.

PS8553.E897T73 2009   jC813'.6   C2008-907391-6

At Ronsdale Press we are committed to protecting the environment. To this end
we are working with Markets Initiative (www.oldgrowthfree.com) and printers
to phase out our use of paper produced from ancient forests. This book is one
step towards that goal.

Printed in Canada by Marquis Printing, Quebec

For my aunt and uncle,
Stella and Don Basso,
who have always been there for me

ACKNOWLEDGEMENTS

I wish to thank the knowledgeable and helpful staff of
the McCord Museum, the Centre d'archives de Montréal, the
Kahnawake Library and La Grande Bibliothèque, especially
Anne Marie. I am also grateful to Margaret and Joe Gardiner, who
hosted me during my stay in Montréal. Every attempt has been
made to preserve the historical accuracy of the events surrounding
the Quebec Bridge collapse of 1907 and the Laurier Palace
Theatre fire of 1927. All characters are, however, fictional.

Chapter One

THE BOY STANDING on Jolene's grandmother's front porch was drop-dead gorgeous. Handsome enough to choke Jolene's voice halfway to her lips so that she could only emit a hoarse, whispery, "Yes?" His eyes — bright and intrigued — with irises as black as the pupils themselves, regarded her curiously. "Yes," repeated Jolene, more clearly.

"I'm Stephan," said the stranger in a deep, resonant voice that reminded Jolene of the beat of a drum. "Rose invited me for supper."

Jolene stepped backwards over the colourful spirals of Grandma Rose's welcome mat, opening the door wider. "I'm Jo," she stammered, "Rose's granddaughter."

Stephan smiled a slow knowing smile. "Actually," he told her, stepping inside, "we met five years ago. Our mothers are good friends."

Jolene's mind raced. Stephan. A friend of her mother's. An invitation from Grandma Rose. "You're Mirette's son," she said as her memory ordered and assembled her thoughts.

"We spent a week at a cabin together in northern Quebec. I was so envious of you."

"Envious? How come?"

"You're a twin. Your brother's Michael, right?" Jolene nodded and he continued. "I'm an only child and I've always been virtual schooled because we've travelled so much. I didn't know many kids then and you were the first twins I'd ever met."

Jolene fidgeted with the door handle. No matter how hard she tried, she could not recall a handsome, envious boy at a cabin years ago. "I . . . I'm sorry, but I don't remember," she confessed closing the door behind Stephan.

"Don't worry," he said. "I looked a lot different back then. I wore glasses and I was pretty scrawny, too."

Jolene stole a glance at Stephan's broad shoulders and powerful torso. His thin t-shirt did little to hide the definition of his rippling chest and stomach muscles.

"I, uh, I row now," said Stephan gesturing towards his chest. Jolene blushed and Stephan's cheeks blazed. "I, uh, I meant the writing," he said quickly, "on my t-shirt, not my . . . uh, I was looking at yours — your shirt, I mean and . . . ."

River's Edge Rowing Club read Jolene silently, focusing on Stephan's shirt before glancing down at her own navy blue top whose bold yellow lettering read, *A Perfect 10*. "Uh, it's a gymnastics shirt," she blurted out, folding her arms across her chest. "A ten's a perfect score."

Stephan jammed his hands into his jeans pockets. Jolene stared at his runners, conscious of the fact that her cheeks were a hot crimson. A strained silence enveloped them. Jolene shifted from one foot to the other and glanced up. A smile played on Stephan's lips. Jolene chewed on a grin, and suddenly they were giggling like two embarrassed teenagers.

Grandma Rose, a tall, elegant, silver-haired woman with an apron tied around her waist, appeared in the entrance way as if their laughter had summoned her. "Stephan," she said warmly. "Come in." She ushered him into the living room and gestured towards Jolene's mother and father. "Supper will be ready in a few minutes, but perhaps you remember these strangers even though it's been quite a few years since their last visit."

Jolene saw her mother wince, but quickly recover. She studied her grandmother's wrinkled face, the piercing blue eyes behind her gold-rimmed glasses, and the thin-lipped smile that her mother had not inherited. She hoped that her grandmother's remark had been more light-hearted than it had sounded. It had been six weeks since Jolene had seen her mother. Six weeks since she, Michael, her dad and grandfather had embarked on a research trip across Canada in a recreational vehicle, leaving Mom behind in Calgary to fulfill her duties as a math professor at the University of Calgary. This afternoon, Mom had flown into the Montreal airport to spend some time with them, and the Thanksgiving holiday with her own mother at her childhood home.

"Hello Mrs. Fortini," said Stephan to Jolene's mother.

She rose and embraced him. "Please call me Kate. You've grown so much since I've seen you. Are you fifteen now?"

"In January."

Jolene did some quick calculations. That made him thirteen months older than her.

"It's nice that you could be here for Thanksgiving," Stephan said.

"Yes, it is," agreed Mom. "I've been busy with graduate students up until now and . . . well you know how it is." ‧

Stephan nodded and Jolene was reminded of the fact that both Stephan's parents were professors — busy, travelling professors.

Dad greeted Stephan with a friendly handshake and then introduced Grandpa. "This is my father, Victor Fortini. Dad, this is Stephan."

Grandpa's dark green eyes twinkled above his moustache. "It's nice to meet you."

"Stephan is the son of my best childhood friend," explained Mom. "Mirette and I grew up together."

"Ah yes, Mirette. I believe I've seen an old photo of the two of you having an accidental mud bath." Grandpa winked at Stephan. "I should have brought it along. Good blackmail material."

"That was the summer both our families went on the ranch adventure and your horses got stuck in that swamp." Grandma Rose sighed loudly. "Those were such delightful days when there was family around."

Jolene's mother dropped into a recliner chair as if she'd been punched in the stomach, and Jolene's heart sank.

"I hear that your parents are in Brazil," said Dad quickly, addressing Stephan, "and that their research is going very well."

Mom darted a glance at Grandma Rose. "Of course good research and presentations are very time-consuming," she added.

Stephan murmured his agreement. Grandma Rose removed her glasses and polished them furiously. Jolene stared at the ceiling, a deep sense of foreboding stealing over her.

"Mom and Dad will be back Wednesday afternoon," Stephan told them. "You'll still be here then, won't you?"

"We plan to be," replied Dad. He settled onto the couch beside Grandpa and carefully smoothed the crocheted coverings that blanketed the couch's upholstered arms. Everywhere Jolene looked there was evidence of her grandmother's needlework — intricately stitched petit point, embroidered runners and crocheted doilies. A half-quilted square of sapphire-coloured irises protruded from the wicker sewing basket near Dad's feet. "I've got some research to do into the Quebec Bridge collapse of 1907 for my museum," said Dad.

"That's right!" exclaimed Stephan. "Rose told me that you'd opened a Museum of Disasters. I think that is such a cool idea — preserving destruction." He pulled a straight-backed wooden chair from around the dining-room table and straddled it, resting his elbows on its wooden back. Jolene marvelled at the muscles in his biceps and forearms.

"It's a lot of work, but the museum's slowly taking shape," said Dad proudly. "And this bridge disaster exhibit has the potential to be fantastic."

Stephan's eyes narrowed thoughtfully. "I thought that the bridge collapse was in Quebec City."

"It was," replied Dad, "but many of the men working on the bridge were from a First Nations reserve just outside of Montreal. They were the Kahnawake people, belonging to the Mohawk nation."

"Really!" Stephan's voice rose excitedly.

"The Mohawk people have a reputation for being some of the best steelworkers in the world," explained Dad.

"Hey Stephan!" greeted Michael, descending the staircase and making Jolene wonder why everybody but she seemed to know the handsome stranger. Michael handed the ginger-coloured kitten in his arms to his sister. "Speaking of food," he continued although nobody had mentioned it, "is supper almost ready? I'm starved."

Grandma Rose bustled into the kitchen, muttering some-thing about interruptions, with Mom on her heels. Jolene remained where she was, stroking the kitten's white paws and stealing glances at Stephan.

"Are you finished your science project?" Dad asked Michael.

"Almost. It would help if the cat wouldn't sit on the keyboard."

Jolene rubbed Chaos' ears affectionately then set him down on the area rug. Immediately the kitten padded towards the sewing basket, batted its handle, and sniffed curiously before jumping in amidst the quilting materials. He re-emerged with fluffy batting stuck to his whiskers.

"Michael, you've got another twenty minutes or so before supper. Keep working," advised Dad

"Yeah, yeah," groaned Michael, disappearing into the kitchen.

Dad shook his head. "How can twins be so different? Jolene's project was a week early and Michael's is a week late."

Jolene shooed Chaos out of the sewing basket and the kitten ducked beneath the couch. "I wish Michael would finish up with the laptop so I can check my e-mails," she said.

"I doubt if Grandma has wireless since she doesn't have a computer," replied Dad, lowering his voice.

"You can use mine," offered Stephan. "We're renovating our house right now so we're living at my grandmother's old place, just next door."

"Why don't you go now," suggested Dad. "There's probably time before supper."

With an inexplicable anticipation building within her,

Jolene followed Stephan to the narrow house next door. Winding wrought iron staircases led to each of the three levels, whose distinct doorways suggested they had once been separate flats. Stephan climbed to the second storey and Jolene did the same. She had visited this same house with Grandma Rose on her last visit to Montreal, and she had a sudden vision of Stephan's grandmother, Claire, with her round little body and heavy French accent. Claire, who had also been Grandma Rose's best friend, had passed away in the spring.

The side-by-side houses were almost identical on the outside — red brick homes with peaked garrets, wooden shutters and iron railings surrounding the balconies. But on the inside, they were a study in contrasts. The rooms Stephan led her through were decorated with carved furniture, symmetrically woven rugs, and paintings and sculptures that spoke of Asia, Africa, Latin America and Europe.

"It looks like you're all settled in," observed Jolene as Stephan started up more stairs.

"My grandmother lived here for fifty-two years," he replied. "You accumulate a lot of stuff in half a century." He smiled sadly. "It took me a long time to get used to being here without grandmaman, but it would be impossible to live in our own place with all the renovations going on right now."

They continued their ascent in silence, Jolene carefully piecing together the information she'd acquired in the last twenty minutes. "How come you're not in Brazil with your parents?"

Stephan's fingers lingered on the railing. "I didn't want to go this time. It's a long way for a short stay and I've been before." He paused on the second floor landing. "It was nice of your grandmother to offer to look in on me and feed me suppers, or I wouldn't have had the option to stay." He continued up a tiny staircase, ducking so as not to hit his head.

"Where are we going?"

"My room's in the attic." He grinned at her with an irresistible smile. "I moved up here a few weeks ago when we finally got around to cleaning it out, and it's awesome." He flung the door open and Jolene stepped into the airy room.

Beams of sunshine streamed through a skylight, illuminating the azure blue of the walls. The ceiling sloped steeply on one side and a large window overlooked the tiny front lawn. Stephan's bed sat against the wall on the high side of the room opposite his desk, with his laptop open. A computer-generated portrait of a First Nations chief, with story-telling eyes and a feathered headdress, was tacked to the wall. Jolene's eyes drifted to the ceiling where dozens of computer-generated eagles dived, flew, swooped and glided. "Are these yours?" she asked in awe.

"Yeah." Stephan hurried towards the closet and pulled the doors open. Hangars scraped right and left. "Come and see this."

Jolene stayed where she was, her feet rooted to the spot by Stephan's strange enthusiasm for his closet. He gestured for her to join him again, and this time she reluctantly crossed the hardwood floor. A crudely drawn tree had been painted on the back wall of the closet. Limbs branched off both sides, ending in broad leaves where names had been recorded in an ornate script. "It's a family tree," observed Jolene, "painted on a closet wall."

"My grandfather did it," said Stephan, pointing towards a signature beside the tree's roots. He tapped the first leaf at the top of the tree. "That's my great-grandfather."

"Eugene Duplessis," read Jolene, deciphering the writing.

"He died before I was born, but when we cleared out the attic, I found this and started researching my genealogy."

"Why is there another smaller tree beside his name?" It was a simple tree with large roots and an eagle perched on a branch.

"It's the tree of peace," replied Stephan eagerly. "A tall white pine with four white roots that point north, south, east and west." He glanced down at Jolene with eyes that glowed with pride. "That tree is a symbol of the Great Law that binds six First Nations groups together in a peaceful way of life." His voice dropped and Jolene felt the silence swell with anticipation. "I'm descended from the Mohawk people, one of those six nations."

Jolene's eyes followed Stephan's fingers, which trailed past leaves bearing the name of his parents to a leaf on the bottom left. Inside, in new paint, was the name Stephan Lacroix.

"Wow," Jolene murmured, grappling with the surprises that were Stephan and looking around as if seeing his room for the first time. It had a distinctly aboriginal theme — in its colours, its simplicity and its decorations. Feathers, dangling from a dream catcher suspended from the ceiling, moved as if in a dance orchestrated by the breeze of the open window. Jolene reached for them, but the plumes spiralled away from her outstretched hand. She'd read about dream catchers, a device that filtered dreams, retaining only the good ones. "Didn't you know about your ancestry before this?"

"Nope. My mom remembers my grandfather telling her when she was a little girl, but she never really gave it much thought. He died when she was a teenager, and as far as she knows, she never met any of her First Nations relatives. But his marriage certificate states that he was from the Mohawk nation."

Jolene studied Stephan's straight white smile, his tanned skin, the black hair that reached almost to his shoulders and his proud expression. He was descended from one of Canada's original inhabitants. Maybe that explained the endless intrigue of his eyes.

"The laptop's on," said Stephan. "Go ahead and check your e-mail. I'll get us a drink."

Jolene watched him leave the attic room. There was something strange and alluring about his enthusiasm, or spontaneity, or naivety. She wasn't sure which. As the sound of his footsteps receded, she slid into his desk chair and logged onto her e-mail account. Ellie had sent her three messages, and she opened the most recent one first. *he did . . . and I said yes. I'm so xcited!!!!!!* Quickly, Jolene opened Ellie's original message, skimming the first few lines of greeting until she reached the real news. *there's a rumour at school that chad's going to ask me to the hallowe'en dance. can u believe it. sandra says curt told her and curt's pretty tight with chad so . . . X your fingers.* Flicking rapidly to Ellie's second message, Jolene filled in the gaps. *chad asked me if i was staying to work on the dance decorations tomorrow night and i told him yes. do u think that means that he's going to ask me to the dance then? how many times have we imagined that? me going to our first junior high dance with chad and you going with gerard. of course u aren't here to go but i'm sure gerard would ask u if u were.*

Jolene smiled at the screen, hit reply and typed. *I am sooo xcited for u.* Ellie had had a crush on Chad since grade five and now she would finally get to go out with him. She wondered what her friend would wear, how many costumes she would try on between now and then, and what she would do with her hair. Jolene returned to her message, but her initial excitement was rapidly giving way to a pervasive sorrow. It was hard being so far away from friends. She missed them and she missed out on things, like her first junior high school dance. Would Gerard have asked her to the dance if she'd been there? Jolene wasn't sure. They had exchanged a few e-mails since she'd left, but he hadn't had much to say in any of them, and he hadn't responded to her last two. If truth be told, she wasn't even sure if she would have said yes if Gerard had asked her to the dance. Still, it would have been awesome to be there. Sorrow seeped through her body, leaving her feeling dull and heavy, lost and weary. *More later* she wrote before signing off. As she hit the send button, Jolene felt a profound emptiness fill her.

Stephan pushed aside the door, carrying two glasses of amber liquid that sparkled in the sunlight and crackled on ice. "Iced tea," he announced, then stopped in his tracks. "Everything okay?"

Jolene accepted the curved glass from his hand. "Yeah," she said slowly. "I just miss my friends."

Stephan leaned against the desk. "That's the hard part about travelling," he admitted. "And one of the reasons why I don't want to go with Mom and Dad anymore." He took a long drink and Jolene did the same, feeling the cool liquid refresh her. "I'm hoping that when my parents return, I can talk them into letting me go to a real school here in Montreal for the rest of grade eight."

His words made Jolene imagine how lonely Stephan's life must have been. But surely jet-setting around the world made up for that loneliness.

"I've met lots of great people in Brazil and Thailand and Russia, all over the world," he said, as if he'd read her mind, "but we never stay long enough to make real friends." He tilted his head to look out the skylight. "Sometimes I just think it would be so cool to have to fill out a late slip, or get changed in a sweaty locker room, or swap lunches with a friend." He sighed. "Just the other day," he said, softly chinking the ice against his glass, "I was wondering what it would be like to take a girl to a school dance." He continued to gaze out of the skylight, his dark eyes seeking sunny dreams.

Jolene glanced at the dream catcher that twirled in the breeze. Stephan was a year older than she was. Why would he ever consider taking her?

Chapter Two

JOLENE TOOK THE STEPS two at a time, skipped past the peach-coloured bathroom, her wall-papered green room, and swung around the doorframe of the sunshine room. Catching sight of her mother at the window, she opened her mouth, but quickly closed it without speaking. Kate reached up to wipe a tear from her eye, and Jolene padded across the worn champagne-coloured carpet. "Mom, what's wrong?"

Her mother swivelled, and then turned abruptly towards the window again. "Nothing," she said, hurriedly dabbing at her eyes. She turned back to Jolene, her eyes smudged with mascara. "Is your dad ready to go?"

Jolene nodded, but the sight of her mother's anguish pained her. "This is about you and Grandma, isn't it?"

Tears erupted and Mom plunked down on the pale-yellow duvet covered with quilted tulips. "I'm sorry, Jolene. I haven't seen you for so long, and now here I am acting like this instead of enjoying my own family."

Jolene sat down next to her. "Grandma's family, too."

"I know." Mom pressed a tissue against her eyes. "And it isn't like I don't try, but I can't seem to do anything right."

"Was it always like this?"

"No." She rose, returning to the window. "My parents were so supportive while I was here at McGill. When I applied to graduate school in Calgary, they were sad to see me leave home, but they were excited for me, too." She paused. When she resumed speaking, sadness had replaced the nostalgia in her voice. "And then my father died in the spring." She looked up at Jolene with eyes that pleaded for understanding. "And everything changed."

"What do you mean?"

"My mother didn't want me to go west. I was the only child still at home and she pleaded with me to stay on at McGill. She claimed that she couldn't bear to live in this big, old house alone. She said she couldn't manage on her own." Mom laughed bitterly. "Look how well she's done. There's nothing your grandmother couldn't do." She wiped a tear from the corner of her eye and continued with her story. "There was a professor who had agreed to take me on as a graduate student in Calgary, and I really, really wanted to go." She bowed her head. "I don't think your grandmother has ever forgiven me for leaving."

"You're not Grandma Rose's only child," Jolene reminded her.

"I know, but then I met your dad and we got married and settled in Calgary. When I had you and Michael, things got a little better. Mom flew out to help when I came home from the hospital. It was so nice to have her there."

"And then?"

"I received my appointment at the university. We got busy. You and Michael had your activities, and Grandma Rose said she was too old to fly anymore. She wanted us to visit at Christmas and Easter and during the summer, and we did, a number of times, but it was expensive and we wanted to go other places, too." She crossed the room and leaned against the doorjamb. "Now every time I talk to her, she lays the guilt trip on me. That just makes me call and visit less often. Then I feel even more guilty."

Jolene could see her mother's dilemma, but the whole thing reminded her of a silly schoolgirl argument. "She's already in her eighties, Mom. Couldn't you just talk this over while you're here?"

"I keep promising myself that I'll do just that. But then she starts with the digs about family and visits, and it just makes me angry. What am I supposed to apologize for, having my own family in Calgary?" Mom blew her nose. "Besides, she's older — isn't she the one who's supposed to be wise and forgiving?"

Despite her mother's anxiety, Jolene couldn't stifle a laugh. "At least I know where my stubbornness comes from," she said, rising and giving her mother a hug. "From both you and Grandma."

While Mom collected her purse, Jolene stepped into the hallway, studying a small staircase at the far end. "Does that go to the attic?"

"Uh huh. Why?"

"Do you think Grandma Rose would let me go up there?"

Mom laughed. "Probably, but you're likely to find more dust than treasures." She ruffled Jolene's hair. "You can ask her tomorrow. Right now, I'd better find Dad so we can get the RV over to the garage for servicing."

Outside, Jolene set Chaos down in the dispersing light and breathed in the velveteen softness of dusk. She stretched out on her back beneath the canopy of crimson leaves that shrouded the maple tree in Grandma Rose's front yard, pulling the hood of her jacket up to cushion her head. The kitten set off exploring, pouncing on invisible bugs and frolicking in the long grass. Despite Mom's anxiety, it had been a good day. Jolene's mother was here after a long absence. Her two remaining grandparents were with them, and for the first time in six weeks Jolene actually had her own bedroom. Chaos reached up onto the maple's trunk and scratched with his tiny claws. Michael was watching a hockey game on television with Grandpa, Mom and Dad had taken the RV to the garage, and Jolene could still hear, through the open window, the rhythmic rocking of her grandmother's chair as she quilted.

Content, she watched the sky change from peacock to rose to tangerine above the silver streak of the distant winding river. A sparrow twittered in the overhanging eaves and Jolene closed her eyes, recalling Stephan's undeniable excitement as he showed her his family tree.

"The sky's prettier from up here."

"Stephan?" She arched backwards to see him leaning over his balcony, then rose and climbed the iron staircase to stand beside him.

"I used to hate sunsets," he told her.

"Why? They're so beautiful?"

"When I was little, I thought that the sun crashed into the horizon every night and that the colours were the result of that great shimmering orb breaking apart."

Jolene giggled and a smile illuminated Stephan's face. "My parents still call it a suncrash."

Jolene loved the way that almost nothing embarrassed Stephan, the way that laughter erupted from him with no warning, the way that he shared the essence of himself without feeling vulnerable or stupid.

"You're lucky," he said, interrupting her thoughts.

"Why's that?"

"Your family's so close."

Jolene thought of her conversation with her mother that afternoon — the ongoing feud with her grandmother. "Have you ever heard my grandma talk about my mom?" she asked on an impulse.

"Sure," he said. "She's so proud of Kate's accomplishments."

"Really?"

"Yeah. Why?"

Jolene considered telling Stephan about her discussion with her mother, but decided against it. There was no point skewing his view of either Grandma Rose or Mirette's best friend.

He shifted soundlessly. "Listen," he said. "Do you hear that?"

Jolene listened to the night.

"It sounds like a baby crying." Stephan peered over the railing into the yard.

Jolene strained to hear better. The cry was faint, almost like a purr. "Chaos!" she cried. "I brought the kitten out with me." Scrambling down the stairs, she searched for the ginger-coloured cat, calling his name. Within seconds, Stephan was beside her. As they entered the perimeter of light that streamed from the house's windows, a loud meow made both of them look up. Chaos was perched high on the branch of the maple tree, his white paws illuminated by the light of a second-storey window, his bright green eyes glowing amidst the rustling leaves.

"Oh no," breathed Jolene. "I bet he's stuck."

Stephan put both hands reassuringly on her shoulders. "We'll get him down. Don't worry."

They strode to the base of the tree, calling to Chaos, but the kitten only responded with worried meows. He was almost half-way up the enormous tree, and had crawled part way out on a limb. His plaintive cries grew louder and more desperate at the sound of Jolene's voice.

Jolene examined the tree. The bark was fairly rough, but the first branch was a long way up, which would make scaling the bottom part difficult. After that, there were enough limbs to make climbing relatively easy. "Shall I boost you?" offered Stephan. "Or would you rather I get a ladder and go up?"

"I'll go," she said. "But it's a long way to that first branch."

Stephan interlocked his fingers and Jolene placed her foot in them and her hands on his shoulders. She was surprised by how easily he lifted her. Gripping the trunk, she extended an arm upwards, but she was still a good half metre short of reaching the first branch.

"Hang on," said Stephan. "I should be able to boost you high enough if you're on my shoulders." Supporting her foot with one hand, he squatted, repositioning himself beneath her. Slowly, he stood, grunting with exertion and propelling her upwards. Jolene's right hand gripped the branch and, with only a slight struggle, she pulled herself up so that her foot was wedged between it and the trunk.

"Thanks," she called down. Deftly, feeling her way, and talking continually to Chaos, she navigated up the maple tree. Lying with her belly against the bark, she stretched towards the terrified kitten. He refused to budge, despite her coaxing. Gradually, carefully, Jolene inched her way along the branch. Just a little farther and she would be able to reach him. Crack! The sound made Jolene freeze. Then it came again. A soft splintering sound. She could feel the branch bending, its bark ripping where the limb joined the trunk. Chaos protested more loudly. The branch bowed in slow motion, then seemed to stabilize.

"Are you okay?" called Stephan. "I think you'd better come down."

Desperately, Jolene stretched towards the kitten. Chaos' body trembled; his claws gripped the shredded bark at his feet. Jolene extended her body as far as she dared. Her fingertips brushed Chaos' fur. Just a little . . . the branch gave way with a sudden snap. Jolene tumbled through leaves and branches, her arms flailing in the darkness. A shriek lodged in her throat. But before she could scream, strong hands gripped her and Stephan caught her against his body. She looked up at him through a screen of leaves and twigs. "Wow. I've never had a girl fall for me like that," he joked, setting Jolene gently down on her feet.

Jolene brushed bits of leaf from her hoodie, unable to respond while his hands still supported her. Instead, she searched anxiously for Chaos. "Did you see the cat?"

A steady purr drew her eyes downward. Chaos stood at her feet demanding attention, obviously unscathed by his fall from the tree. Jolene scooped him up and held him tightly against her.

"Cats bounce better than we do," said Stephan, plucking a twig from Jolene's hair.

"Definitely," she agreed. She glanced up at his dark, attentive eyes. "Thanks for catching me."

"Any time," replied Stephan. "Any time."

Jolene buried her face in Chaos' fur. There was something about Stephan that disarmed her — something that made her feel both welcome and vulnerable. An outside light flickered and Jolene heard her grandmother open the front door. "I'd better go," she said. She would clean up the branches tomorrow in the daylight.

Stephan paused on the first stair leading to his balcony. "Goodnight, Jo."

"Goodnight, Stephan." As she followed her grandmother into the house, Jolene had to admit that it had been a good night, a very good night.

But the goodness of the night didn't last. From upstairs, between cold, pressed sheets, Jolene heard her parents return. The front door had hardly latched shut when her mother called into the kitchen. "When's the last time you had your car serviced, Mom? It sounds like it hasn't seen a mechanic for years."

"That car's fine as rain," replied Grandma Rose. "Besides, what would a mathematician know about mechanics?"

"Enough to know that it's not safe to drive. It sounds like . . ."

Jolene rolled away from the argument, away from the open door, wondering when it would end. When Grandma Rose died? If Mom felt guilty now, what would that be like? She sat up and rearranged the pillows.

A faint knock sounded on her door and her grandfather peeked inside the room. "Are you still up?"

"Who wouldn't be?" retorted Jolene. "With all that arguing downstairs."

Grandpa sat on the edge of the bed. "They're a lot alike, your mother and grandmother."

"I'll say," agreed Jolene, giving in to her mounting frustration. "Both stubborn and strong-headed."

"Yes," agreed Grandpa with a laugh. He patted Jolene's shoulder beneath the quilt. "Don't worry about it, Jo. They'll work it out."

"I doubt it. For years now it's been like this."

Grandpa looked momentarily surprised. "They're both clever, strong women. They'll sort things out," he repeated.

Jolene snuggled deeper under the covers. "I hope so, Gramps. I sure hope so."

Chapter Three

THERE WAS NO FAMILY tree painted on the wall of Grandma Rose's attic, but layers of dust covered an old dresser with a cracked mirror and stacks of forgotten books. A floor lamp with a bare bulb guarded a splintered kitchen chair, a footstool with stuffing protruding from its seams, and a stack of old sports equipment — tennis rackets with frayed strings, a pair of cross country skis and two unlaced baseball gloves. On the far wall, beside a sink and stove, was an empty alcove where a refrigerator might have been. Beside the kitchen nook, a door led to a tiny bathroom. "This used to be a bachelor suite," said Grandma Rose sneezing and waving her long, delicate fingers in the air, "although we never used it as such." Carefully, she picked her way through piles of boxes. "It's mostly junk up here now."

"It's gorgeous and sunny," said Jolene, admiring the sloped ceiling and pecan-coloured hardwood. "If I lived here, I'd turn it into a bedroom, like Stephan did." Jolene wandered among the boxes, trailing her fingers across dust-covered memories. "What's in this?" she asked, standing beside a small blue metal trunk in the corner beneath the window.

"Why, I'd forgotten that was here," admitted Grandma. She grabbed an old shirt hanging on the corner of a box and wiped the trunk's lid clean of dust. Kneeling, she forced the metal clasp open and lifted the lid. The clean, pungent smell of mothballs assaulted Jolene's nose.

Jolene reached into the trunk and extracted a bundle of clothing. The first garment was a long, black wrap-over style coat with an enormous button to fasten it on the side and a shawl fur collar. As well, there was a shimmering bronze sleeveless dress with a scalloped hemline, a chocolate brown bell-shaped cloth hat, and heeled gold shoes with pointed toes and criss-crossing straps.

Grandma Rose's face shone as she took the silky dress from Jolene. She held it up and played with the sash that fell from two bronze bands around the waist. "This was your mother's."

"Mom's?" asked Jolene. "I didn't know they wore that style when she was young."

"They didn't," said Grandma Rose. "I made this dress for a drama production set in the 1920s that your mother was in when she was just a little older than you. But the hat, coat and the shoes are authentic. They were my mother's and we used them because they were a perfect fit." Her eyes glistened. "Oh, Kate looked lovely on stage, and she pulled off her part so beautifully. We were so proud of her."

Witnessing such genuine emotion, Jolene wondered how things had changed so much between her mother and grandmother. Grandma Rose handed the garments back to her. Her nostalgic look had been replaced by her usual practical expression. "I'd best go eat and get ready."

"Where are you going?" asked Jolene with her hands full.

"I promised to work the quilting bee at the Heritage Fair today." Without another word of explanation, Grandma Rose disappeared into the stairwell.

"Wait!" cried Jolene. "Can I bring some of these things downstairs?"

"Whatever you like, dear," replied Grandma Rose. "As long as you put everything back where you found it when you're done." Her voice descended the staircase while Jolene quickly closed the trunk and, clutching the bundle of clothing and new memories of her mother, followed her grandmother.

Dad was halfway through his peanut butter toast when he suggested that they all go to the Heritage Fair with Grandma. Mom and Grandpa were keen, Jolene wanted to see Grandma Rose's quilt entry, and Michael was persuaded by the fact that the fair was on the old Expo grounds where the midway was a permanent fixture.

"Can we invite Stephan?" asked Jolene, hoping nobody would see it as an odd request.

"Of course," said Mom. "Run next door and tell him we're leaving in half an hour."

"There's no point taking the car," advised Grandma Rose. "There's a bus that goes directly to the fair and parking is impossible and expensive."

"By the time we pay bus fare for six people," said Mom, "it would be cheaper to drive."

Grandma Rose turned and regarded her daughter defiantly. Jolene skipped out the back door before the argument began.

Stephan was happy to join them. When they returned together, Grandpa and Dad were assembling change for the bus. Jolene stole a look at her mother whose expression was distant and sullen.

"There wasn't room for all of us in the car," whispered Grandpa to Jolene.

Outside, Jolene felt her earlier anxiety evaporate like the dew on the grasses. A day out might put things right. Maybe it would remind Grandma and Mom of earlier days. They would reminisce, laugh together, and realize how silly their disagreement was. Perhaps Grandpa's prediction would come true.

A shiny Ferris wheel, the Drop of Doom and the narrow

rails of a roller coaster towered above the fair site. Jolene inhaled the sugary smell of cotton candy mixed with the aroma of cinnamon-dipped doughnuts as they disembarked from the bus. The piercing screams of riders intermingled with the brass notes of a trumpet and the shuffle of footsteps. Riding the motion of the crowd, they filed through the turnstile and huddled together under the Canadian flag at the south entrance. After agreeing to meet up at three o'clock, the adults headed towards the pavilions that housed the old-fashioned fair and the children ran to line up for the rides.

Music blared, cars spun, riders screamed at every twist and turn. Jolene, Stephan and Michael raced through the grounds, letting each ride take their breath away until talk of the next one restored it. Finally, after being spun in both directions, repeatedly turned upside down and catapulted through the air, they went in search of a cold drink. The lemonade booth was just outside the quilting exhibit, and Jolene was keen to see Grandma Rose's quilt. Sipping lemonade, they passed ladies in long skirts and bonnets churning butter, and laughing farmers milking goats. Most of the people helping at the exhibits were close to Grandma Rose's age. Their faces were creased by age, but their hands moved with youthful speed.

When they reached the quilting display, Jolene watched her grandmother's fingers push and pull a needle to create small, uniform stitches on a large quilt. It was stretched out on a huge wooden frame; at least three other women worked on it simultaneously, their voices rising and falling in time with their needles. "It's beautiful," offered Jolene, coming to stand beside her grandmother's shoulder. The boys were right behind her.

Grandma Rose introduced them to the quilting ladies. "Your dad and grandfather went to see the printing press next door, and your mother is over looking at the home-made dolls," she told the twins. She leaned towards Jolene as the boys went in search of Grandpa and Dad. "There are some cute dolls, but none as special as the one your mother made when she was your age. It had the most amazing face, that doll did — as if she would speak to you at any moment."

Jolene found her mother who immediately grabbed her arm and pulled her back towards the quilts. "Come and see this." They stopped in front of a quilt whose primary colours arranged in an ornate spiralling geometric pattern reminded Jolene vaguely of a solar system. "It's called an Antikythera mechanism and it's based on an ancient Greek pattern." She smiled proudly. "It's Grandma Rose's."

"Really? It's gorgeous."

"Spectacular," agreed Mom.

"Did you tell her that?"

Mom gave her an uncomfortable look. "She's busy quilting," was all she said.

By the time they caught up with the boys and Grandpa, Dad was no longer with them. "He's over there," said Grandpa, nodding towards a desk in the corner of the exhibit. "The gentleman who runs the press has an old newspaper collection and he's been kind enough to share them." Jolene could see her father poring over the documents. Her grandfather, unable to resist a good story, was perusing a book of memoirs.

Stephan was seated on a nearby bench, completely absorbed in a newspaper when Jolene plunked down beside him. "Hey," he said, "look what I found." He closed the single paper copy and Jolene stared at the headlines. *Kahnawake Reserve Mourns Following Bridge Collapse.* Her eyes darted to the date, *1907*.

"How many men were killed?"

"There were eighty-six men on the bridge that day; seventy-five of them died and thirty-two of those were Mohawks."

Mom and Michael joined them. "Grandma Rose will be finished in another half-hour. I'm going to wander through the old car exhibit," said Mom. She pointed at a nearby tent where two antique cars were parked in the doorway.

"They have an old Model T Ford and a Durant's Star from the 1920s," Grandpa informed her.

"If there are any more rides you want to do, you should probably head out now," Mom advised them before leaving.

"I'd like to ride the Drop of Doom," said Jolene excitedly.

Michael shook his head. "Count me out. I'll go check out the cars."

Jolene looked hopefully at Stephan. Her brother was terrified of heights but she didn't want to go alone.

"Sure," agreed Stephan. "Let's go."

They hurried back onto the midway, but the lineup for the Drop of Doom was huge, snaking its way through the fairgrounds as far as they could see. "Let's try the Ferris wheel," suggested Jolene. Stephan was unusually quiet as they dodged children carrying enormous stuffed dinosaurs and munching on corn dogs. "You okay?" Jolene asked.

"I was just thinking of how it must have been for the people on the Kahnawake reserve after the bridge accident."

"Talk about being surrounded by grief. I wonder how long they mourned?"

"I don't know," said Stephan. "I wonder how they ended up as steelworkers in the first place."

"Next," called the midway attendant, and Jolene and Stephan scrambled onto the gigantic metal wheel. It rose sporadically as other riders loaded, giving them a panoramic view of the fairgrounds, the wharves and freighters, the Jacques Cartier Bridge, and in the distance, Mount Royal. When they reached the top, Jolene shifted so that she could see in all directions. The white dome of the Olympic Stadium with its elevated arm raised like a huge antenna was visible behind her.

"Michael doesn't like heights," she said, "but being up high makes me feel free."

Stephan took a deep breath. "I love heights," he told her. "They make me want to fly and dive like an — "

"— eagle," finished Jolene. "Is that why you have dozens of eagles on your bedroom ceiling?"

Stephan grinned. "To the Mohawk people, the eagle is the messenger of the Creator." His voice was soft and respectful. "Eagles can see the past, present and future at a glance and are a powerful symbol of courage." He hesitated for a moment. "Last week, I'm sure one followed me alongside the river."

"Followed you?"

"It flew directly over the bike path where I was riding, almost as if it was escorting me, until I turned off to go home."

"You must have been on its flight path."

"Maybe." The Ferris wheel began its circular course, its movement blowing Stephan's hair over his shoulders.

Jolene felt her stomach drop as the Ferris wheel began its rotation, accompanied by the high-pitched whir of the motor. "Do you know any Mohawk people?"

"No. I wish I did."

They whizzed over the striped canopy of an ice-cream kiosk. "It's neat to find out about your ancestors," said Jolene. "I'd like to find out more about Grandma Rose's family." She slid her hands along the metal safety bar as they plunged backwards over the top of the circle. Her left one bumped against Stephan's, and he leaned towards her until their shoulders touched.

"You should make a family tree," he advised. "I can help, if you wish."

"I wish," said Jolene, making Stephan smile. Inside her head, feeling the pressure of his shoulder against hers, Jolene finished the sentence in silence, then let the ride ferry her away into her dreams.

Chapter Four

JOLENE WAS TIRED and thirsty by the time the bus reached Grandma Rose's stop. Grandpa, with the book of memoirs he had purchased tucked under his arm, was discussing the antique cars he had seen. Jolene dropped back to walk alongside her grandmother who had fallen slightly behind. "Tired, Gram?"

"A little," admitted her grandma, but she quickened her pace. Soon they had caught up with Stephan. "I really ought to stop in at the church on the way home," Grandma Rose told Jolene. "One of the altar cloths needs some sewing repairs."

"I'll wait with you," volunteered Jolene.

"Me too," said Stephan. "I'm in no hurry."

Jolene ran ahead to tell Mom of their plans and then waited up for Grandma Rose and Stephan. When the others turned left, they continued towards Ontario Street and soon reached a stately stone church with a towering, rectangular steeple on one side. Above the wide steps, a statue of the Virgin Mary rested between the wooden maroon doors on the front façade. *L'Église de la Nativité de la Sainte Vièrge* said the brass nameplate on the wall. Stephan swung one of the doors open and Jolene peered inside the dark interior. Beams of light, stained by coloured glass, decorated the pews. But after being outside in the late summer warmth, the dark cool made Jolene shiver.

"We'll wait outside," she said.

"Okay, but it might take me a few minutes to find Father Leonard." The door clicked behind Grandma Rose, and Jolene and Stephan traipsed back down the steps.

"Hey!" exclaimed Stephan, pointing at a corner store across the street. "How about a slurpee?"

"Awesome idea."

"I'll get them. You stay here and wait for your grandma."

As Stephan crossed Ontario Street, Jolene followed the walls of the church, tracing the rough stone with her fingers. At a corner of the steeple, she paused and watched Stephan enter the convenience store. Then she continued into the steeple's shady recess. A strange sensation came over her. The shade was warm and the air inside it felt as if it had been electrically charged. Catching her breath, Jolene stepped deeper into the shadows. They grew darker, denser, almost alive. Jolene whirled around, her heart hammering as the warmth intensified. This was not a normal shadow created by the concrete pillar blocking the sun. It was a time crease, a means of travelling through time into the past. She was certain.

Jolene hesitated. It was Grandpa who had first introduced her to time-travel, and she had already had a few historical adventures with him. The memories flooded over her. Scenes from the past — her dresses and hats, the sounds and smells of coal towns, wharfs and markets, and most of all, the faces of new, old friends flashed before her. Not all her memories were pleasant ones, but the lure of history tugged hard at her. She had promised her grandfather not to time-travel alone, but he wasn't here with her now. If she just slipped back for a minute . . .

Taking a deep breath, she took a single step farther. Immediately, she felt the increased pressure of having entered a portal in time. Her limbs felt as if they were being elongated, her chest heaved in an effort to breathe, and drops of sweat formed on her forehead and throat. Struggling against the force of the crease, Jolene felt as if she were being stretched like an elastic band. Then suddenly a rush of hot air sent her staggering forward, hurtling into the past.

Montreal lay ahead of her. Skiffs of snow dotted the dirt street in front of the church. It was her grandmother's church, only its stone façade looked cleaner and less weathered. Square buildings, their faces dotted with dozens of small windows, surrounded it, and a car resembling the one Grandpa had pointed out earlier at the fair was parked on the street at the base of the church's steps. Had she just arrived in the 1920s?

Voices reached her and Jolene caught sight of a group of boys playing street hockey. A shot ricocheted off the wooden power pole on the corner. The boys wore knickers and knee-length socks, with sweaters or matching jackets. Two of them wore caps with wide brims. Creeping forward, aware that her jeans and hoodie were not appropriate attire for this era, Jolene hid behind the car. She wouldn't stay long.

Two girls, dressed in long wrap coats, resembling the one she had found in the attic, and fuzzy gloves were coming down the road. Jolene ducked down out of sight, then rose just enough to watch the girls through the car's windows. One of them wore a close-fitting cloth hat pulled well over her eyes, but the other was bare-headed, with short, dark hair. She looked in Jolene's direction and Jolene gasped. Quickly, she sank to the ground, unable to believe what she had just seen. Looking at the dark-haired girl had been like looking at her own reflection in a mirror.

A shout rang out and Jolene peeked through the car's windows again. The dark-haired girl ran towards the vehicle to retrieve the boys' ball and Jolene studied her features. She could have been her twin. Quickly, Jolene shrank back out of sight as the sound of footsteps approached. The boys shouted and the girls shrieked. They bolted from the car with the boys in pursuit, and as they did so, Jolene saw the girl with the hat drop a small black clutch purse. Stepping from her hiding place, Jolene picked up the purse. She'd never catch up with the girls now, but perhaps she could leave it in a place where they would find it.

The doors of the church gaped. Voices escaped. Jolene panicked. Still gripping the purse, she darted towards the steeple and into the time crease. Immediately she felt the hot tingle of the crease envelop her. Her body was stretched and strained as the light gave way to darkness and she was hurled into the present, losing her balance and landing on the ground, right at Stephan's feet.

"Where did you come from?" he asked. He was holding two slurpees, watching her with incredulous eyes. "You weren't here a minute ago."

"Stephan, I can explain," said Jolene, but her grandmother's voice reached them at the same instant. Quickly, she stuffed the purse into the pocket of her hoodie.

"I've got the cloth. I hope I didn't keep you waiting too long," said Grandma Rose, waving a plastic bag at them. "Slurpees! What a good idea," she added, seeing Stephan.

Jolene pried her slurpee from Stephan's hand. "It was Stephan's idea," she said, meeting his gaze, which was a mixture of amazement and fear. "I'll explain later, I promise," she whispered, as she fell into step with her grandmother.

Her words seemed to release Stephan from his trance, but the incredulous look remained in his eyes.

"Grandma Rose," said Jolene, her thoughts racing from the past to the present and back to the recent past. "I've been thinking of creating a family tree while we're here. Stephan's offered to help me." Stephan's eyes, although fixed on her face, gave no indication that he had heard her words.

"I'm sure I've got some old photos that might interest you. In fact, there were some very old things of my mother's in a shoe box," said Grandma Rose.

"Did she die recently?"

"No, many years ago, when I was just a baby. My stepmother sent the shoebox after my father passed away."

As they reached the front door, Jolene watched her grandmother climb the concrete steps, placing both feet on each stair and steadying herself with the hand rail.

"Aren't you coming in?" Grandma Rose asked.

Jolene looked sideways at Stephan, who was watching her with expectant eyes. "I think we'll finish our slurpees outside."

Stephan let out a deep breath as the door closed. "Okay," he said, "start talking."

"Can we sit?" asked Jolene. "Maybe on your balcony?" She wasn't keen to be overheard by anyone, especially not Grandpa.

Seated on the lounge chairs on Stephan's balcony, Jolene's thoughts somersaulted through her head. "Back there at the church," she said finally, "I was hiding." Stephan's eyebrows arched in disbelief. "Just around the corner where . . ." The hurt expression on his face cut Jolene's lies short. She got up and attempted to pace in the narrow space. He said nothing, patiently waiting. Desperately, she studied his broad cheek-bones and oval face. It was a face that she could trust, a face that would know if she didn't tell the truth. "Okay," she began, "this is going to sound unbelievable, but it's true."

Stephan looked skeptical.

"Years ago, my great-great grandfather was a physicist in Italy. Gramps now has his journals, and apparently he discovered a way to time-travel." Jolene forced her words out more quickly than ever. "He knew that time is a continuum, kind of like a long ribbon. According to the theory of continuum mechanics, which actually exists, all the points on that ribbon, whether they belong to the past, present or future, have the same properties. I don't really understand it all, but that means that past, present and future are all really one." She glanced up at Stephan's dubious stare, then averted her eyes. "Anyway, energy isn't a continuum, and so if there's energy from some big historical event, it can crease this ribbon of time. Gramps calls them time creases and they look like hot shadows." She stopped pacing and dared to look at Stephan. "There's one by the church. I went through it into the 1920s, I think."

Stephan crossed his arms over his chest and Jolene felt her heart fall. He didn't believe her. Why should he? She hadn't believed Grandpa when he'd first told her either.

She sat down beside him. "I know it sounds absurd, but it's true. So far on our cross-Canada trip, I've already time-travelled to 1903, 1917 and 1913."

"Really?"

Jolene tried to ignore the sarcasm in his voice. "Yes, really."

Stephan crushed his empty slurpee cup. "So if I asked your grandfather, he'd tell me this is all true?"

"Yes," said Jolene, "but you musn't do that." Stephan rolled his eyes. "The energy is often from a disaster, so it can be dangerous to go back. Last time, in Ontario, we got ship-wrecked in a horrible storm. He'd be furious if he knew I'd gone back in Montreal, especially alone."

Stephan rose, a sad look in his eyes. "I'm so disappointed," he said candidly.

"Stephan, please, you have to believe me." Frustrated, Jolene jammed her hands into her hoodie pocket, her fingers bumping against the purse she had collected during her brief trip through the time crease. "Look," she said, withdrawing it excitedly. "One of the girls I saw in the past dropped this."

She handed him the purse and he returned to his chair. Carefully, he unlatched the small metal clasp and reached inside, removing a clean handkerchief embroidered with the initial S. Jolene fought the urge to dump the clutch purse upside-down. Instead, she watched as Stephan methodically removed a comb and then an envelope. Written on the outside was the name *Suzanna Dumont*, followed by the address *63 Rue Darling*. "Suzanna must be the name of the girl who owns this," said Jolene. "That's why the handkerchief has an *S* monogram."

"That street actually exists," said Stephan. "It's not far from here." He opened the envelope while Jolene held her breath. It was empty.

"Is there anything else inside the purse?"

Stephan's large hands disappeared into the handbag, feeling from one end to the other. "Nope," he said, but his eyes contradicted his words. Slowly he extracted three coins, turning them carefully over in his wide palm and scrutinizing them carefully. "1921, 1923, 1919."

Jolene leaped to her feet. "You see," she said. "I told you."

"This purse could just belong to someone who collects old coins," Stephan said quietly, but there was no conviction in his words. "Except I know for a fact that you materialized out of thin air at the church, and . . ." He studied Jolene's eyes. "You always struck me as honest." His fingers closed over the coins. "Tell me again about these time creases."

Happily, Jolene explained for a second time. When she had finished, Stephan re-opened his hand and regarded the coins. "That's amazing!" he said. He smiled at her for the first time since they had left the church. "That's absolutely unbelievable!"

Only Jolene knew that he did believe her. "You know what's really amazing?" She didn't give him time to respond.

"The other girl, the one who didn't drop the purse . . . that girl looks exactly like me."

"What? Are you sure?"

"It was like we were twins, Stephan. You wouldn't have been able to tell us apart."

"You already have a twin."

"I know, but she looks like my identical twin."

"Wow! What did she say when she saw you?"

"She didn't see me. I hid behind an old car." Jolene gestured at her clothes. "I'd have been a bit conspicuous dressed like this."

"I suppose," agreed Stephan. "How old was your look-alike?"

"I'm guessing my age."

Stephan was still perplexed. "Are you sure you were in Montreal?"

"Positive. Grandma Rose's church was there, in the same spot as it was today. That's the way time creases work. To time-travel, you have to be in the place where the crease was formed."

"So does that mean you can go back again?"

"Yes." Jolene's eyes sparkled. "And I really should return this purse. I do have Suzanna's address."

Stephan frowned. "Didn't you just tell me that it can be dangerous to go back, especially alone?"

"That's true," admitted Jolene. "It would be a good idea to know what happened at the church in the 1920s."

"Jo! Stephan!" Grandpa's voice boomed across the neighbourhood. "Supper's ready."

"We can research it after supper," said Stephan as they headed down to Grandma Rose's. "I guess this isn't exactly dinner table conversation, is it?"

"No," Jolene agreed. "It would be great if we could keep it our secret."

"Okay," he agreed, winking at Jolene, "then it's our secret."

Jolene fought the urge to hug him. There was something wonderful about sharing a secret with Stephan. There was something wonderful about sharing anything with Stephan.

They joined the others at the table. Grandpa was quiet as they dished up and Jolene watched him with interest. "I read a fascinating book about a young Mohawk man during the early 1900s," he told them.

Jolene recognized the sound of a story. An idea, like a tiny drop of water dripping from a frozen waterfall, had seeped into her grandfather's consciousness. High in the crevices of his brain, a trickle of thought had begun, which would gradually gain momentum and flow into a story.

"Jimmy was a skywalker," began Grandpa. "He walked in the sky. Nimbly, he crossed the steel girders suspended high above vast waterways. Jimmy worked alongside his father who, with unwavering patience, had first watched him climb the bridge near the Kahnawake reserve in Montreal." Grandpa smiled at Stephan. "For months he had practised scaling the beams, traversing the girders with precision and balance.

Even then, as a teenager, it had seemed a most natural movement, Jimmy's supple body bending and swaying like a firmly rooted tree. His uncle had called him 'little sapling,' adding that he was a 'born skywalker' and Jimmy was inclined to agree.

"High above the ground, Jimmy felt his heart lift, his bones lighten, his feet skim the surface of the beams. Not once in his eight years of working as a steelworker had he lost his balance, tripped or teetered. Yet, again and again his father had counselled him to confront the fears that lay within him. Only a fool, he said, would not be afraid of falling from such dizzying heights. He advised Jimmy to identify the shape of his fear so that he might know it and how to defeat it before it defeated him. For fear would, his father promised, visit him one day."

Grandpa paused to twirl his moustache. Hardly a utensil moved and Jolene noticed that nobody was actually eating.

"One August day, from amidst the clouds, Jimmy looked down at the bear of a man that was his father and recalled his warnings. Fear had found his father many years ago when Jimmy was just a child. It had arrived in the form of a dark, ferocious wolverine whose claws gripped the steel beams and whose fervent eyes paralyzed his father hundreds of metres above the ground. For nearly an hour his father had stood in the shadow of the demon while his friends and co-workers had quietly, from a distance, called encouragement. At first, in the presence of the unrelenting creature, their words had gone unheeded, but slowly as the sun had reached its zenith, Jimmy's father had heard the animal spirit that had first spoken to him as a young man — the lumbering black bear. Across the girders it came, its massive head swinging back and forth, sniffing and grunting as it advanced towards the wolverine. At first, the demon held its ground, fire in its eyes, but suddenly the black bear reared and, with a decisive swipe of its paw, sent the creature hurtling towards the ground. Standing on its hind legs, like a man, the bear then spoke to Jimmy's father, instructing him to place his feet in its paw prints. And when Jimmy's father looked down at the steel beam on which he stood, he saw that the metal had been indented with bear tracks. Without hesitation, he followed his animal spirit to safety."

Grandpa sipped from his water glass and the family resumed eating, quietly, expectantly.

"The memory of that story made Jimmy envy his father on that sunny August afternoon. Like all young Mohawk men, he understood that the black bear had come to his father four times in a significant way during his life, thereby making a lasting connection between their spirits. Jimmy, raised on the reserve that now bordered the city, had no animal spirit. There were few wild animals in the area, and Jimmy counted himself lucky that his house was backed by a stand of trees that two red squirrels called home. He had slowly won their trust when he and his wife had first moved in three years ago. When he returned home on the weekend, he and his two-year-old daughter, Marie, would feed the squirrels peanuts. Marie loved the tickle of their tiny paws as they took the nuts from her soft palms. His wife was expecting their second child, and Jimmy wondered if it would be a brother or sister for Marie. A co-worker's voice interrupted his thoughts and Jimmy picked up a bucket of rivets and prepared to cross the girder on which he was working.

"With the beam stretching before him, Jimmy was suddenly aware that a cloud had blocked the sun. He wasn't sure if he saw it first or sensed it — the icy gust that waited at the other end of the beam, but its presence halted him abruptly. Like the first frosted winds of fall, it advanced towards him, its icy breath freezing the blood in his veins like sap congealing. Jimmy, the 'little sapling,' once so lithe and supple, had grown into a mature tree, and his sturdy trunk and extended limbs offered more resistance to the wind, making him more vulnerable. The air swirled mercilessly around Jimmy's head, chanting his daughter's name, piercing his heart with fear. He stood immobile at the top of the bridge — alone.

"Below him, his father looked up and saw his paralyzed son. At first, the wind jumbled his father's words, scattering them like brittle leaves. It slashed at Jimmy's limbs, gusted about his feet and stole his cap, driving his long hair into a mad, blinding frenzy. In that momentary darkness, his father's words found him. 'Look inwards,' they told him. Jimmy's mind tried to conjure up the massive form of a bear or the snarling face of a wolf, but the wind swept the images from him. 'Turn inwards.' Jimmy focused on himself — his trunk, his roots, his limbs — and suddenly he felt the delicate touch of tiny paws. A red squirrel, its bushy tail raised, scampered across his foot. Its wire-like whiskers twitched as it smelled the air and then quickly scurried towards the wind. Furious, the wind attacked with an intensity that threatened to break the strongest tree. The squirrel flattened itself against the girder, streamlining its body, tail and ears so that the wind merely glanced off its back and sheared over the edge of the beam. While the wind re-gathered itself, the fuzzy rodent scurried forwards, then sensing a second assault, flattened its belly against the rail. The wind hollered threats, drove itself into the girders and dropped angrily into the atmospheric abyss below. Again and again, it attacked, provoked by the simple defence of the agile squirrel. By the time the creature had reached the opposite end of the beam, the wind had depleted itself so much that it could only spin in harmless exhausted wisps. The squirrel, seated on its haunches, chattered at Jimmy, who, now, without hesitation, lifted his right foot and started across the horizontal beam. Out of the corner of his eye, he could see the squirrel leaping playfully from girder to girder with an ease and agility that restored Jimmy's confidence."

Jolene felt her lips curve upwards in a smile. Grandma Rose laughed, a soft contented laugh and Stephan beamed.

"Jimmy would never forget the day that fear found him while he was walking in the sky," concluded Grandpa. "And

the red squirrels in Jimmy's back yard would never understand why they were given extra peanuts each and every
weekend from then on."

Chapter Five

JOLENE SLID THE wet dishcloth over the rack and slipped away from the conversation in the kitchen. Stephan had excused himself after supper, and she was anxious to see what he had discovered. She sped up the steps to his front door, where he met her, wearing a frustrated expression. "I can't find much on the internet about the church, except that it was destroyed by fire in 1921. But one of the coins came from 1923, so that doesn't make any sense."

"Don't worry about it," said Jolene. "I was going to start my family tree tonight. Care to join me?"

Stephan waved his left hand, and only then did Jolene realize he was holding the phone. "I need to make a call first," he told her. "But I'll come over when I'm done."

"Okay," said Jolene, wondering why this news came as such a surprise. She backed towards the steps as Stephan closed the front door, then turned and descended. Whom did he have to call right now? What couldn't wait? A dull uneasiness came over her, but she pushed it aside as she entered the house and went in search of her grandmother.

She found her in her bedroom. "Up there!" declared Grandma Rose, pointing to the top shelf of her bedroom cupboard. "The old albums are in that box."

Jolene scrambled onto the chair and dragged the old cardboard box forward until it teetered on the edge of the shelf. Carefully, she let it fall into her arms. Grandma Rose helped her down from the chair and she hustled off to the dining room where she had already assembled a large piece of bristol board, and had drawn two boxes which would bear the names of her maternal great-grandparents.

The album covers were cracked and peeling, but as she lifted them, a black and white photo slid to the table. Jolene picked it up, studying a newly married couple. A tall, slender woman robed in white stood next to a stocky, heavy-jowled man whose barrel chest threatened to burst the buttons on his vest. The bride was slightly taller than her husband with delicate features beneath her veil — high cheekbones and dark eyes that seemed to speak to the observer. Her body was poised as if she might silently glide out of the picture at any moment, and the bouquet of flowers in her hands appeared more wild than cultivated. Jolene glanced quickly at the woman's husband, feeling a sudden incongruity between his staunch reliability and the whimsical, breezy nature of the bride.

"That's my mother and father," Grandma Rose informed her, coming to stand behind her shoulder. "On their wedding day."

Jolene flipped the photo over. It was dated, *September 24, 1917.*

"Imagine getting married in the middle of harvest," clucked her grandmother.

Jolene studied the man's large hands and thick shoulders. "He was a farmer?"

"All his life. Every Sunday he wore a suit to church and always looked just as uncomfortable as he does in this photo."

Jolene didn't want to talk about her great-grandfather. It was the woman in the photo who intrigued her. "Tell me about your mother."

Grandma Rose sighed. "I'm afraid I can't tell you much," she said. "She died when I was just nineteen months old."

"What happened?"

"I don't really know," said Grandma Rose. "The doctors never diagnosed her with anything in particular, but my brothers tell me that she started to die the day I was born."

"She got sick in childbirth?"

Grandma Rose shrugged. She flipped the photo album open and turned a few fragile pages before stopping at a photo of two young boys perched on a stack of hay bales.

"Those are my brothers, Gus and Edward," she said gesturing at the freckle-faced boys. "Gus was eight when I was born and Edward was five. Normally Gus would have been at school, but he was home with a cold the day I entered this world."

Despite her longing to know every detail, Jolene said nothing in the ensuing silence. Her grandmother had returned to a place where she had once lived, a place that Jolene, if she were patient, would soon be able to visit through her grandmother's words.

"Apparently, she was washing up lunch dishes. Papa had gone out to the barn." Grandma Rose's eyes had paled to a soft blue. "Edward was playing on the kitchen floor with a toy car he'd got for Christmas." Another momentary pause. "The phone rang and mother answered it. Gus doesn't remember much except that she suddenly cried out, slammed her fist against the wall and slumped to the ground crying 'No, no, no!' Gus went running to the barn and returned with Papa. Mother was sobbing, clutching her belly, the receiver dangling in the air. Father took her to the doctor's and a day later I was born. I should have been a Valentine's Day baby, but instead I was almost five weeks early." Grandma Rose smiled at Jolene, as if she'd suddenly remembered she had an audience.

Jolene asked the question that hung on her lips. "Who was the phone call from?"

"According to Gus, Papa asked and asked her, but she refused to answer him." She smiled weakly at Jolene. "I was, of course, too young to remember any of these conversations."

"What happened after that?"

"The doctors couldn't figure out why she'd gone into labour early. But from that moment onwards, she was never the same. Edward said that she used to sit and hold me and I'd be screaming and she'd just be sitting and staring out into space, as if she couldn't see me or hear me."

Jolene wondered how an infant felt to be invisible.

"At first the doctors thought she might be suffering from depression — often new moms get kind of depressed and moody — and that it would pass as she took care of me and watched me grow. But her mood never changed. She shut herself away on my birthday and she never came out again."

"Came out?"

"I don't mean literally. She did some chores around the house — laundry, dishes, cooking meals — but she rarely talked, never went off the farm, and the neighbour ladies told me that her eyes always looked empty after I was born. She died when I was nineteen months old, but no cause of death was ever determined." Jolene's grandmother chewed on her bottom lip.

"That's awful," said Jolene, staring at the beautiful bride in the photo.

Grandma Rose nodded and for a moment Jolene thought she saw guilt flicker in her eyes. "It wasn't your fault," she said adamantly.

"I suppose," said Grandma Rose, lifting the photo from

Jolene's fingers. "I just wish I could have known her. What I do know of her, I learned through my brothers. Papa re-married shortly after she died. He needed a woman to look after us kids and to keep the house." She handed the photo back to Jolene. "I can tell you, though," said Grandma Rose looking at the boxes Jolene had drawn on the bristol board, "that Papa's name was Claude Renaud and mother's maiden name was Nora Richardson." She watched as Jolene pen-cilled in the names. "And my stepmother was an English woman, Mabel Hastings. She was our neighbour's sister and was widowed in the war."

Jolene debated about adding Mabel's name to the family tree, but decided against it. Instead, she used her ruler to draw three more boxes under those containing her great-grandparents' names. She filled them in with the names of Rose and her two brothers, along with their birth dates.

"Do you know anything about your grandparents?" she asked Grandma Rose wondering how far back she could trace her heritage.

"My father's parents were farmers as well, but they both died in the Spanish flu epidemic of 1919. As for my mother's family, I don't know much." She drummed her fingers against the wooden surface of the dining room table. "I meant to look for those old things of mother's that Mabel sent."

Before Jolene could respond, Grandma Rose had left, her mind preoccupied with the past.

Jolene returned to the photo album, pausing beside a picture of her great-grandmother Nora rocking an infant. The picture was dated 1927. The infant must have been Grandma Rose. What had happened the day Nora had died? What devastating news had come by telephone? From whom? Questions piled on questions until Jolene could no longer see past the stack of them. Looking for answers, she continued to flip pages, stopping when a second wedding photo appeared. A round woman with a large nose and a firm jaw smiled out from beneath a coarse lace veil — Mabel. A slightly older Claude looked out with the same no-nonsense expression he'd worn in his first wedding photo. Jolene studied Mabel's appearance. There was nothing coy or whimsical about the woman. She appeared to be determined, tough and sensible — a much better match for the sturdy Claude.

Jolene positioned the two wedding photos side by side. She was descended from the graceful bride with the vivacious eyes. The thought pleased her.

The doorbell rang. Jolene set the photos aside and went to answer it, but Stephan had already entered before she reached the door. "Sorry I took so long," he said in a breathless voice. "What did you find out?"

Jolene led him towards the dining room table. "Grandma Rose told me about her parents and brothers, and she found a couple of old photo albums."

Stephan reached for an album and Jolene huddled beside

him as his fingers turned each page. There were pictures of
the children at various ages and stages, church picnics, her
great-grandfather sitting on the hood of an antique-look-
ing car, farmers harvesting, and groups of strangers dressed
for formal and informal occasions.

Jolene picked up the first wedding photo she'd found.
"That's my grandmother's mother and father," she explained,
anxious to share her discoveries. "My great-grandmother
Nora started to die the day Grandma Rose was born."

Stephan's long eyelashes blinked down at her. Slowly, trying to recall all that Grandma Rose had told her, Jolene related the details of her grandmother's birth and her great-
grandmother's death.

"And nobody knows who telephoned that day?"

"Apparently not, but I've been wondering if . . ."

"If," prompted Stephan.

Jolene scrutinized the photo again. "Do you think she
might have been in love with someone else?"

Stephan's eyes widened.

"I mean, if someone had called to tell her that her lover
was dead, killed or had left her . . . well, maybe that would
have been enough of a shock to bring on childbirth!"

"What made you think of that?"

Jolene shrugged. "They just look so different, as if they
came from different worlds." She picked up the second wedding photo. "This is my great-grandfather's second wife.
Doesn't she seem a better match for him?"

Stephan inhaled, his forehead furrowing in contemplation. Finally, he let out a long breath. "I can't say I follow your logic, but anything's possible, I guess."

Jolene scowled at him. This was romance. There was no logic, was there?

Stephan inclined his head close to hers. "Come to my place," he whispered in her ear. She lifted her chin, gazing into his eyes and he leaned closer still. "I want to show you something I found on the internet."

Jolene felt an unexpected letdown. "Sure," she agreed. "I'll just tell Grandma Rose." As she climbed the stairs, she wondered what she had expected him to say. And why did he always surprise her?

Chapter Six

UPSTAIRS, STEPHAN motioned for her to sit in his swivel chair. "I wanted to show you this," he said, tapping the "enter" button to bring his laptop out of hibernation.

"Doppelgänger," pronounced Jolene, reading a bold red encyclopedia entry aloud. "What's a doppelgänger?" But her eyes were already perusing the online entry as she asked the question.

"It's a German word that means literally 'double walker,'" Stephan told her, "but it's used to refer to any double or look-alike."

"You mean like the girl I saw in the past."

"Perhaps," said Stephan, "but I hope not."

"Why?" She let her eyes scroll down. The word was also

used to describe shape-shifters in folklore and fantasy games.

Stephan's index finger touched the screen part way down the page. "Doppelgängers are typically associated with bad luck and evil," he read softly. "A doppelgänger seen by a person's relatives portends illness or danger, while seeing one's own doppelgänger is often an omen of death."

"Death?" Jolene pulled her knees up to her chest, resting her feet on the seat of the chair. "What else does it say?"

"That some doppelgängers cast no shadow and have no reflection in mirrors or water." Stephan took a deep breath and continued, "And that they are often associated with time-travel and parallel universes where the doppelgänger is actually the doubled person but from a different time era or universe."

Jolene spun the chair so that she faced him. A tightness, like a fist being clenched, had formed inside her. It left her cold, as if she had just encountered the air that precedes a winter storm. "You don't believe this folklore nonsense, do you?"

Stephan's black eyes reverted to the screen. "There are all kinds of historical accounts where people see these evil twins and then bad things happen to them." He straightened up and began to pace about the room, his head brushing the feather that dangled from the dream catcher. "Queen Elizabeth saw her double on her bed and died shortly thereafter."

"Everybody dies at some point, and the queen was old by then," said Jolene.

"In Norse mythology, a doppelgänger precedes a living person and is seen performing their actions in advance."

Despite the apprehension she felt, Jolene laughed. "This all sounds like science fiction."

Stephan flopped down on his bed. "Yeah, well so does your time crease. First you time-travel and now you have an evil twin — and apparently both are dangerous." He turned anxious eyes to Jolene.

She swallowed a smile. He was worried, concerned that something bad would happen to her. It was such a sweet thought. "I'll be fine, Stephan," she reassured him. "I've time-travelled before."

"And almost died in the process."

"I don't even know if I could die in the past," she told him gently.

"Yeah, well, I'd rather you not find out now."

Rising, Jolene crossed the room and perched on the bed next to him. "I really want to go back, Stephan. Just once more, to give Suzanna back her purse and to see if the girl really is my double." She paused. "Maybe I was wrong. Maybe up close, she won't look like me at all."

"You seemed so sure earlier."

"There was a resemblance, but maybe there's some other explanation."

"Like?"

Jolene took a deep breath and voiced the thought that had occurred to her many times since she had first seen her double. "Maybe she's some distant relation of mine."

"I suppose," said Stephan. "It's just so weird. You being able to time-travel and having an evil twin."

"Are you referring to Michael?" joked Jolene.

A smile inched across Stephan's face, pushing up one corner of his mouth before nudging up the other. Jolene felt the taut feeling inside her begin to release. "When are you planning to go?" he asked her.

"Tomorrow."

Worry turned Stephan's smile upside down. "They say it's dangerous to try and communicate with a doppelgänger."

"Stephan," said Jolene evenly, "I'm not even sure if I'll see her again. I only know where Suzanna lives."

"Can I come with you tomorrow, to the church?"

"I'd like that," said Jolene, but his question had started her mind spiralling away in another direction — wondering if, by any remote chance, Stephan could accompany her back in time. Could he time-travel? Others outside her family had, but not everyone possessed the ability. Her father couldn't. Could Stephan? She said nothing more, except to arrange to meet him in the morning.

Jolene awakened to the sound of Grandpa's laughter. She had dreamed of her look-alike and the image of herself looking at her other self. She caught a glimpse of her real self in the mirror and was relieved to see only one of her.

Without bothering to change out of her pyjamas, Jolene

stumbled downstairs where Grandpa and Grandma Rose were busy making pancakes. "Now if it had been twenty years ago . . ." said Grandma.

"Morning, Jo," Grandpa called catching sight of her. "Hungry?"

"A little," she said, clambering onto a stool. "Where is everyone?"

"Your parents are out for a jog and Michael is still asleep."

Jolene glanced out the window. Clouds obscured the morning sun, dulling the lustre of the dew-soaked leaves. As she watched, one gigantic leaf detached itself and parachuted decisively to earth.

"It's supposed to rain," said Grandma Rose. "What are your plans for today?"

"Stephan and I were planning on . . . uh, having a look around the neighbourhood."

Grandma Rose held her pancake flipper in the air. "Good."

"I saw your family tree," Grandpa told Jolene. "That should be an interesting project and this is a good place to do it."

"That's what I thought," said Jolene. "Did you ever find that shoebox, Gram?"

Her grandmother's flipper waved back and forth. "No, and for the life of me, I don't remember where I put it."

The back door opened and Jolene's parents entered, sweat glistening on their foreheads. "There's rain coming," said Dad. "You can feel it."

While Mom went upstairs to shower, Jolene set the breakfast table and then returned to her own room to get dressed. She heard Michael's heavy steps in the hall and then Mom's lighter ones. "Mom," she called, throwing her door open, "come and see what I found in the attic."

On her bed, she had laid out the 1920s dress, coat and hat that she had found yesterday. Her mother's face broke into a wide smile. "Why look at this," she said, picking up the garments. Her pale blue eyes shone. "Your grandmother made that dress for me when I landed a minor role in the school play. It was set in the 1920s and I was a flapper." Jolene let her mother speak, even though she knew the story. "The drama department thought they had costumes for all of us, but in the end, nothing fit me. Your grandma sewed the dress in less than a week and all for my three and a half minutes on stage." She laughed then frowned. "She was so stressed, but I bet you've heard all about that already, hey?"

"Not at all," said Jolene, picking up her brush and tugging it through her shoulder-length hair. "Grandma just told me about how great you looked in your costume and how successful the play was."

Mom looked surprised. "Both you and Michael need haircuts," she said, changing the subject.

"I want to let mine grow," Jolene called after her mother. As Jolene put her earrings in, she wondered how two people could live through the same events and remember things so differently? That was a question that needed more thought.

But thought was superseded by plans as the family gathered around the breakfast table. Dad had made arrangements to meet with a First Nations professor at McGill University, Michael wanted to go swimming at the campus pool, Mom wanted to do some errands and check her e-mail, and Grandma was hoping to go to a quilting store. Jolene let Stephan into the front hallway as her mother and grandmother launched into another argument, this time about there being no computer in the house.

"What would I need it for?" demanded Grandma Rose.

"For one thing, we could e-mail."

"I have a phone."

A look of annoyance crossed Jolene's mom's face. "There is a two-hour time difference between Calgary and Montreal," she said, "which makes it difficult to call for business or personal reasons."

Silent resentment emanated from Grandma Rose.

"You're welcome to use our computer," Stephan offered Kate.

Mom thanked him and stomped upstairs to find her purse.

Jolene distracted her grandmother. "What are you looking for today, Gram?"

"There's a new quilting pattern that I saw in a magazine but haven't been able to find. I'm hoping the quilting store downtown has it."

"You know," Jolene said softly so that Mom wouldn't hear, "you could probably order it on-line. Stephan and I would look for you."

"Really?" whispered Grandma Rose.

"Sure," said Stephan. "We'll show you later."

Mom rejoined the others, and Jolene and Stephan watched them go. Now they were free to return to the church, and she was just minutes away from a visit to the 1920s.

"Are you ready to go?" asked Stephan.

"In a minute," said Jolene, bounding up the stairs. Inside her bedroom, she slid the dress on, surprised by how loose and straight it was. The bronze colour made her eyes look darker, a deeper green than usual. The scalloped hem barely reached her knees. Quickly, she removed her runners and pulled on a pair of pantyhose and the gold shoes with the criss-crossing straps. She had tried them on this morning and been surprised to discover that they were a reasonable fit. Next, she drew the coat around her, wrapping the overlay across her body and fastening it with the large button on her left side. The fur collar hid her dress completely. Jolene tucked the cloth hat in her coat pocket, then wrapped her jeans, socks and shirt in a bundle and stuffed it into her backpack along with her flats.

She inspected her image. The shoes and collar might raise a few eyebrows, but she hoped she wouldn't be too conspicuous in the present.

"Wow!" declared Stephan as Jolene descended the steps. "Talk about retro."

Jolene opened her coat and half-twirled as if she were on a catwalk. "How do I look?"

"Fantastic," said Stephan, bringing a blush to Jolene's cheeks.

She proceeded to tell him all about finding the clothes in

the attic. "I brought along my regular clothes, too, just in case everyone's home by the time we get back."

Stephan opened the door and they ventured outside. "How long are you planning to stay?"

"Not long," said Jolene, outlining her plan to him. She would return the purse to Suzanna and try to strike up a conversation with her so she could find out some information about her look-alike. "Any ideas how?" she asked hopefully.

Stephan shook his head. "I'm not very good at drawing girls into conversation." Jolene was going to object, but he seemed preoccupied with another matter. "Jo," he said as they approached her grandmother's church, "do you think you could teach me to time-travel?"

Jolene hesitated. It would be wonderful to time-travel with Stephan, and she had entertained the same thoughts last night. But time-travelling could be dangerous. Still, the yearning in Stephan's eyes was irresistible. "We're not sure if everybody can time-travel," explained Jolene. "Michael and I and Gramps can, but Dad doesn't seem to be able to. It has something to do with his perception of history, we think." Stephan's eyes begged her. "I can try," she agreed finally, watching his face light up.

"Okay," said Jolene after she had relocated the time crease beside the steeple. Clouds had all but masked the sun, but she could feel the hot, electrical air of the crease. "The time crease is just below that window. Hold my hand when you enter it and try to think of yourself as situated in one place while time passes over you."

Taking Stephan's hand, Jolene stepped forward, feeling herself enveloped by the crease. She felt her body strain and then fling forward. The church loomed before her, but she no longer held Stephan's hand. Quickly, she darted back through the time crease, relieved to find him safely in the present. "Try again," she advised, "and don't let go. Instead of travelling with time, let time go by you." But the result was the same. Each time she went through the crease, the pressure within it pulled them apart.

"Never mind," he said when she returned to the present after the third attempt, "but you have to tell me everything."

"Of course," said Jolene, feeling his disappointment.

Stephan's eyes had grown dark and serious. "Are you sure you should go?"

"You were ready to come with me," she reminded him, fully understanding the irresistible pull of time-travel.

"I guess, but I couldn't find out much else about the church."

"Don't worry. I'm not going to be at the church anyway." She took the purse and handed him the backpack. "Where was it again?"

"Two streets north and one to the west."

"Okay. I'll try not to be too long."

"Wait!" said Stephan as she approached the time crease. "Take this!" He handed her his cell phone.

"I won't be able to call from the twenties."

"I know that. It's a camera phone. Take a photo of your double for me."

Jolene tucked it in her pocket. For a moment, Stephan looked as if he would hug her. Instead, he patted her shoulder and wished her luck. "I'll be right here," he promised.

Jolene entered the time crease with mixed emotions, which were soon dispersed by a blast of cold winter air. After drawing the coat tighter around her hips, she withdrew the hat from her pocket and pulled it on, positioning it low on her forehead, similar to the way in which the girl she assumed was Suzanna had worn hers. Patches of snow dotted the dirt roads. Bravely, she followed Stephan's directions, passing two gentlemen on a street corner. They brushed by without noticing her, and Jolene took that as a good sign.

After turning onto Darling Street, she located number 63, the first floor of a large two-storey brick house. Bypassing the iron staircases that wound towards the upper floor, Jolene approached the door. For a moment, her courage wavered. Then, resolutely, she marched up the front steps and rapped with her knuckles.

Chapter Seven

INSIDE THE HOUSE, Jolene heard the patter of footsteps. The door swung open. Suzanna stood shivering in the cold, a perplexed look on her face. "Oui?"

"Uh, hello," said Jolene nervously. She took a deep breath and continued in French, thankful that she had done her elementary education at an immersion school. "Je cherche Mademoiselle Suzanna Dumont." A face became visible over Suzanna's shoulder and Jolene felt her breath fail momentarily. The girl was her double — the one she'd seen on the street with Suzanna. She had the same deep green eyes, the same nose and lips, the same dark hair, only hers was bobbed and Jolene's somewhat longer.

Suzanna had obviously noticed the resemblance because she now stood between them with her mouth agape. "You look like twins," she stammered in English, then addressed Jolene in a mixture of French and English. "Who are you? D'où viens-tu?"

The clenching feeling had taken hold of Jolene's insides again. Mentally, Jolene tried to ignore the things that Stephan had told her about doppelgängers. "Je m'appelle Jolene," she responded. "I'm visiting Montreal from Calgary and I think I found your purse." She reached into her coat pocket and produced the black clutch purse she had found on the road.

A look of joy came over Suzanna's face. "She found it," she shrieked in English, with only a faint French accent.

"That's lucky!" said the dark-haired girl, but she was obviously unnerved by the fact that her double was standing just metres away from her.

"Oh thank you." Suzanna stepped back into the warmth of the house. "Please come in," she said as if suddenly remembering her manners. "I'm so grateful. It was a Christmas present." She smiled at Jolene. "I'm Suzanna, as you know, and this is my sister, Poppy."

Poppy! Jolene felt her knees give way. She stumbled forward, holding onto the doorjamb for support and trying to control her breathing. Poppy was her middle name. She and Michael had been born on Remembrance Day.

Suzanna brushed the purse's soft fabric exterior. "We went

back and searched after we realized I'd dropped it," she explained, "but it was nowhere to be found."

"I'm sorry I didn't return it yesterday. I found it on my way home and didn't have time to deliver it."

"Oh, then you must be staying nearby," said Suzanna.

"Yes," said Jolene.

There was an awkward silence, which Poppy finally broke. "What's your last name?" she demanded, apparently as anxious as Jolene was to understand their strange resemblance.

"Fortini," said Jolene. "My mother was a Tremblay and her mother was a Richardson."

Poppy shook her head. "I'm a Dumont. Suzanna and I are twins."

Twins? Jolene's thoughts ricocheted about like the frenzied dance of an inflated, untied balloon just released into the air. Heat, like a fever, spread across her neck and throat and she unbuttoned her coat. Quickly, she looked from Suzanna to Poppy, then back to Suzanna. There was certainly a family resemblance, and both girls were dark-haired, but Poppy's eyes were a bright green and Suzanna's hazel. "That, that's so strange," said Jolene, hearing her voice crack.

"Yes," agreed Suzanna, "considering you two look more alike than we do."

Jolene raised her eyes to meet Poppy's. "I'm also a twin," she told her. "I have a twin brother named Michael."

"Really?" Poppy was watching her now with an almost suspicious look.

"I know this is going to be hard to believe," continued Jolene, "but Poppy is my middle name."

Suzanna stepped aside and shut the door firmly behind Jolene. The three girls stood in a triangle of strangling silence. Jolene could feel Poppy's fear mixed with suspicion and puzzlement. But she also sensed the girl's inevitable attraction to a mystery. "Well, I guess stranger things have happened," Poppy announced finally, then abruptly added, "Where did you say you were from?"

"We recently came from Calgary, Alberta."

"We don't have relatives there, do we?" Poppy asked Suzanna.

"Not that I know of," replied her sister.

"Unless," began Poppy. "Unless mother had a lover . . ."

"Stop it!" ordered Suzanna. "Mother loves father, you know that."

"I know, but it is an uncanny resemblance."

There was another awkward silence. Jolene shifted uncomfortably from her right foot to her left foot and stared at the straps that covered her stockings. "Well," said Suzanna, linking and unlinking her fingers, "why don't you stay for a bit? If you're new here, you could probably stand to get to know some people."

Jolene smiled gratefully at her. "Thanks," she said. She wiped her shoes, noticing that the girls still wore theirs in the house, and slipped off her coat.

"Oh!" exclaimed Suzanna as soon as she had done so.

"Look at your dress." Her eyes were two full harvest moons. She walked around Jolene, inspecting her with an exhilaration that was palpable. "It's the flapper style," she announced. "Just like in the magazines." She continued to scrutinize Jolene's outfit. "It's fabulous and if you powdered your stockings, they'd look ever so much more nude."

Jolene wondered if she had made a wise choice in her clothing. Perhaps she should have looked into flappers more closely. "It's a pity our mother isn't home," Poppy said, leading Jolene down the hallway. "She'd love it." Jolene breathed a sigh of relief. "Although Papa might not approve of the short skirt." Suzanna giggled and so, too, did Poppy. Jolene squirmed uncomfortably, trying to pull her skirt down and hoping that the twins' father was out. Both the girls' skirts reached past the knee.

They had arrived at a brightly decorated room with two twin beds and matching bubble gum pink curtains. Dresses, skirts, stockings and blouses lay scattered about the room. *Suzanna* read an embroidered plaque on the wall. *Poppy* read another above the second bed. Magazines littered the night table and dresser whose swinging mirror was cluttered with cut-out pictures of models. All wore their hair short and bobbed. Loose-fitting garments covered their thin, boyish frames exposing their arms and legs. Long strings of beads dangled from the models' necks and from the girls' open dresser drawers.

"Now, if Father saw you," Poppy told Jolene, placing her

hands on her hips and lowering her voice to a deep, bass tone, "he'd say, 'That hemline's a little too far from the floor and not close enough to heaven for my liking, miss.'" Suzanna and Poppy collapsed onto the bed, giggling.

Jolene perched on a chair. "Is your father strict?"

"When he thinks he should be," answered Poppy.

"And why would he think he should be?"

"Oh, it's all this talk from the church," explained Suzanna. "The bishops and priests say that the new dancing is immoral and corrupting young people today. They don't like jazz music or the theatres, or anything that is fun." She let her bottom lip protrude in a pout. "Mother says it will all pass though."

"That's because of Mother's background," said Poppy.

Jolene concentrated on Poppy's voice. It was hard for her to look at the girl and see herself, and even harder not to think that her presence in Poppy's life might be a death omen.

"Our mother," explained Suzanna, "was a vaudeville dancer before she got married." Jolene made a mental note to research vaudeville as both girls rose nimbly. Without a word between them, Poppy raced for an old record player. As the needle began to scratch the big, black record, they found space between the twin beds, their toes tapping to the brassy jazz music that filled the room. "Can you do the black bottom?" asked Suzanna, beginning to sway.

Before Jolene could ask what the black bottom was, the girls lifted a foot behind them and brought it down with a hard stamp. This was followed by a double stamp, a step and another double stamp. Soon they were moving, stamping and swinging their hips in a box-like pattern, their arms rising from the floor to overhead. The blare of the brass band intensified and the girls began to swivel their hips, clapping in front of their bodies, then slapping their hipbones. On they went, arms waving, extending upwards and swooping downwards as the foot stamping quickened into a motion that, Jolene thought, resembled tap dancing. Poppy and Suzanna grabbed the hems of their skirts and moved their feet faster and faster as the music peaked, then ended abruptly.

Exhausted and giggling, they collapsed into one another's arms. "We'll teach you," said Poppy between gasps of laughter. Suzanna flopped onto her bed, flushed and joyous.

"That was amazing!" said Jolene. "I've never seen anything like it," she added honestly.

"We just learned," said Suzanna. "Mother taught us after she'd been out one night." She giggled. "And had a few drinks."

"Why is it called the black bottom?"

"Mother heard that it's based on the moves of a cow stuck in the mud," said Suzanna, giggling.

"Mother can dance it fabulously," said Poppy.

"And so can our aunty," added Suzanna. "Well, she's really mother's friend but we call her aunty and she visits once a year. It's so much fun."

"I can hardly wait to teach the girls at school," said Poppy.

She turned towards Jolene. "Will you stay long enough to go to school?"

"I'm not sure."

"Well, if you do, then you'll go to St. Joseph's," Suzanna told her. "That's the school we attend and we start again on Monday."

"That would be lovely," said Jolene, meaning it. For the first time in six weeks, she was enjoying the girl talk that, she realized, she had missed so much. She was close to Michael, she loved her grandparents and parents, but her heart ached for her girlfriends — someone to sit with and chat about whatever was in her heart at the time. Time! She had lost track of how long she'd been in the past and she rose reluctantly, remembering her promise to Stephan. "I should probably go," she told the girls. "But thank you for a lovely visit."

"You'll have to come again," said Suzanna.

"Why don't you join us at the drug store for a milkshake tomorrow?" suggested Poppy. "Then you could meet some of the other girls from school. They'll be so shocked to see how much alike we look."

"I might be able to," said Jolene, "if you tell me where the drugstore is."

The girls did so as they accompanied her to the front hall. Jolene stopped in front of a large photo of a handsome young soldier in uniform. A brass plate beneath the image read *Private Marc Dumont*. "Is this your father?" she asked the twins.

"Our uncle," replied Suzanna. "He was killed in the war."

"I'm sorry," said Jolene, thinking that both girls had inherited his smile. She said her goodbyes and walked until she reached the corner of the house. There, she stopped and surveyed the street. It was empty. Suzanna and Poppy's bedroom window was just metres from her. Slowly, with her back against the uneven bricks, she edged her way back to the window. The girls moved about inside their bedroom. Digging into her pocket, Jolene extracted Stephan's cell phone and positioned it alongside the window frame. Poppy was almost directly in front of her. She pressed the button, saw the red light flash and ducked. Tucking the cell phone into her pocket, she headed towards the church. She had so much to tell Stephan.

But he was nowhere in sight when she emerged from the time crease. Big, fat drops of rain beat down on her cloche hat. Quickly, she pulled it from her head and stuffed it in her pocket. "Jo!" Stephan called her name from the door of a coffee shop across the street and she dashed towards him, trying to escape the rain. "I'm so glad you're back."

Inside, she took her backpack, changed quickly in the ladies' washroom and joined him for a steaming hot chocolate he had just ordered for her. Her drink was cold by the time she was done telling him everything.

"So what year was it?"

Jolene scrunched up her nose. "I'm still not sure although it's definitely the twenties," she said. "I couldn't really ask."

"You might have looked at one of the magazines."

Jolene wished she had thought of that earlier. "Sorry," she said, "but I did take a picture." Withdrawing the cell phone from her back pack, Jolene handed it to Stephan. He rapidly pushed buttons, then tilted his head to scrutinize the image on the screen.

"Let's see," demanded Jolene, sliding her chair around to sit beside him. A slight halo of reflection surrounded Poppy, blurring the picture.

"She does look like you," said Stephan. "Her face is a slightly different shape and she's a bit taller, but otherwise you two definitely look alike." Jolene thought she heard a note of regret in his voice. He continued to scrutinize the photo. "Is there any way," he said slowly, "that she could be you in a different time?"

"How could that be?"

"You might exist in two time periods at the same time."

Jolene shook her head. "I don't think so. It's never been that way before."

"And, as far as you know, you can't bilocate?"

"Bilocate?" echoed Jolene. "I don't even know what that is."

"It's the ability to project yourself into two locations at the same time," explained Stephan. "It's one of those paranormal phenomena that nobody's really sure exists."

"Uh, doubtful," said Jolene.

The rain had tapered off to a soft shower, and Stephan suggested they head home. It was approaching suppertime. "I don't know why, but I just have this feeling Poppy and I must be related," said Jolene, "except I don't see how."

"Well, now that we know Poppy's surname, we should be able to look up information on her at the Archives or maybe even e-mail requests for vital certificates. I'll do that when I get home, for Poppy and Suzanna."

"Thanks," said Jolene, trying to focus on the present. But the mysterious events of the past with their odd coincidences kept pulling her back to the twenties.

Dad arrived home just before supper, with Grandpa and Michael in tow. "How was the meeting with the aboriginal professor?" asked Mom.

"Great," said Dad. "In fact, he invited us out to the Kahnawake Reserve tomorrow."

Stephan, who was helping Jolene set the table, jerked his head up. "The Kahnawake Reserve," he repeated.

"Do you know it?" asked Dad.

"Yes, I mean no, not really," replied Stephan. "I've seen the signposts and read about it but I've never been. My parents promised to take me there when they return."

"Stephan is a descendant of the Mohawk people," added Jolene.

"Really!" Jolene could tell that Dad was impressed. He set his camera bag down on the couch. "You're welcome to join us tomorrow, both of you."

"That would be great! Thank you so much." Stephan dropped a knife with a clatter.

Grandpa frowned. "I believe Kate wants to go, too. I don't have to go along if there's not room in the car," he offered.

"Yes, you do," said Jolene. "You're the museum's resident storyteller and so many of the men who died on the bridge were from the reserve." She picked up Chaos who had come looking for attention. "I'll happily stay home with Grandma Rose."

Dad smiled at her. "Thanks," he said. "Unfortunately, there's only room for five." Jolene wondered if Mom's wanting to go had anything to do with having spent the day with Grandma Rose. "That reminds me," Dad continued, "I'd better give the garage a call and see when the RV will be ready."

Stephan laid out the remaining utensils, while Jolene arranged the glasses. He looked up abruptly. "I wish you were coming tomorrow," he said with a look that made her heart flip-flop.

Chapter Eight

AS SOON AS THE car pulled away the next morning, Jolene turned to Grandma Rose. "So, what shall we do today?" she asked.

"I would like to make pies for Thanksgiving, even if your mother insists that we don't need them."

Jolene let the comment slide, aware that Grandpa had been overly optimistic. Mom and Grandma Rose had not worked things out, nor did it seem likely they would. The tension between them was as tight as a clothesline and their curt words and stiff comments hung like freshly laundered clothes for the whole family to see. There had to be something that she could do to resolve the situation.

Watching Grandma Rose tie her apron on and move about the kitchen, Jolene marvelled at how familiar it all was. So many of her mother's mannerisms were also her grandmother's. So many of her mother's words came from her grandmother's mouth, and yet they believed that they were so different. "Pumpkin?" asked Jolene, referring to the pies.

"Yes," confirmed Grandma Rose, "but with a special recipe."

"Your mother-in-law's?"

"Why, yes," said Grandma, "how did you know?"

"It's the one Mom uses. It's the only one she ever uses."

Jolene noted the astonishment in her grandmother's eyes. "But," Jolene added truthfully, "she says her pies never turn out as tasty as yours."

Her grandmother reached into a cupboard for a glass pie plate, but not before Jolene had seen the proud look on her face. As they worked, Jolene took the opportunity to learn about vaudeville acts. They were, her grandmother explained, popular entertainment in the first two decades of the twentieth century and usually consisted of a combination of entertainers — magicians, acrobats, musicians, animal trainers, dancing girls and comedians. Suzanna and Poppy's mother had been one of those dancing girls.

When the pies had been baked and the kitchen restored to its usual orderly state, Grandma Rose plugged in the kettle. Jolene glanced at the clock, wondering if she might still be able to join Suzanna and Poppy for a milkshake. Despite Stephan's concerns, she desperately longed for the company of girlfriends and to know about her look-alike.

The aroma of pumpkin pie spice filled the air. "Let's have tea and some lunch," Grandma said, but Jolene noticed the fatigue in her voice.

"I'll make it," she replied, slightly surprised when her grandmother hardly protested. Jolene studied Grandma Rose's face as they ate. Although she looked content, she was more wrinkled than she had been the last time they had visited and her eyes seemed more subdued. She looked old.

"I wouldn't mind having a nap this afternoon," said Grandma Rose when they had cleared the lunch dishes.

"Okay," said Jolene, realizing that it was the perfect opportunity to take a quick trip back to the past. "I might go for a walk if that's okay."

"Sure. It's a beautiful day."

"What time will you be up?" Jolene wondered how long she could safely be away before her grandmother worried.

"I generally sleep for a few hours," confessed Grandma Rose, revealing that a nap was a usual part of her routine. "Take a key."

Jolene waited until Grandma Rose's bedroom door was firmly closed before changing into her clothes from the 1920s. The coat was too warm for the day, but luckily there were plenty of unusual fashions in Montreal. Tucking her hat in her pocket, Jolene headed briskly for the church.

A wedding party arrived at the same time as Jolene, delaying her passage through the time crease. She crossed the street and waited at a bus stop, trying to appear inconspicuous until the bride's long white train had swept inside the impressive doors. For a moment, she reconsidered her actions. Stephan would be worried. Grandpa had forbidden her to time-travel without him. But she'd already been safely back once, and she had a real yearning to be with girls her own age, especially Poppy. Quickly, Jolene scampered towards the time crease. The pressure threatened to crush her, before suddenly releasing her into the 1920s.

A car drove up as Jolene materialized in the past, but the driver didn't seem to notice. On the steps of the church, whose tolling bells filled the warm Saturday afternoon air, was another nervous bride, dressed in an embroidered silk gown, cloth-covered shoes and a short veil. Jolene hurried away, smiling at the way times changed but did not change.

As she turned onto St. Catherine Street, the main east-west thoroughfare, a car rolled into an intersection, stopping for a horse and buggy that clip-clopped down the road. There were more cars than horses and the sound of horns and engines coughing made the animals skittish. A feeling of expectation, a feverish din that was as real as the young men and women who strolled past shops and theatres enveloped her.

Jolene watched a group of three young women emerge from a doorway. Their coats were draped across their arms, and Jolene noticed that their dresses although different in colour were all sleeveless, straight, boyish shifts decorated with beads and tassels — somewhat like hers. Their hair, too, was short and sleek beneath their cloche hats, and their faces were adorned with makeup. Two of them smoked, long cigarette holders dangling from their fingertips. They were, Jolene knew, flappers, and having looked up flappers in Grandma Rose's encyclopedia, she knew that both their dress and hair styles marked a shift to the enticing, boyish look of the twenties. The term flapper had come from the way they danced the Charleston, flapping their arms and walking about like birds during the dance. Not all the women on the street dressed like them.

Jolene felt slightly uncomfortable in her mother's costume, certain that her mother had been playing a character older than a teenager. She was grateful that Suzanna and Poppy had not ridiculed her, and glad that her hair was short, although it did not truly resemble the bobbed style most girls her age were wearing. Trying to set aside those worries, Jolene continued up St. Catherine Street. She passed a fire station, a gang of noisy boys playing jacks, and found the entrance to the drugstore. Choosing an aisle, she walked between shelves of epsom salts, liver pills, ointments, toilet paper, shampoo and cod liver oil, heading for the rear of the store where music and voices erupted towards the ceiling. Poppy caught sight of her as she emerged into a small soda shop and waved. Jolene joined her and Suzanna at a table with three other girls. "Want a milkshake?" called Suzanna over the music. "Papa's treat."

"Sure," said Jolene, removing her coat and hanging it on a coat tree behind the booth. When she turned to face the girls, she noticed that they were all staring dumbfounded at her. "What?" she asked, feigning innocence.

A pretty auburn-haired girl finally spoke. "It's just that you and Poppy, well, you look almost like twins." She grinned. "Even though she's already a twin."

"So is Jolene," announced Poppy in a bubbly voice. "Isn't it odd?"

While Suzanna ordered a milkshake for her, Poppy introduced each of the girls in the booth. Jolene greeted them, their eyes scrutinizing her dress and hair, her freckled skin and deep green eyes, with intrigued expressions. And then as suddenly as the conversation had died, it flared again. The girls' chatter filled the booth and Jolene relaxed into its warmth and comfort. How she had missed this.

She looked about the shop. A younger group of boys savoured their ice cream treats at a nearby table. Shoppers came and went and a group of young men and women played the one-armed bandit slot machines beneath a cloud of cigar smoke. Behind the counter, a burly man tightened the lid on a milkshake cup and proceeded to shake the container vigorously. Jolene watched with amusement, as sweat beaded his forehead. Quickly, he drained the cup into a glass, inserted a straw and brought it to her. Jolene sipped the frothy drink.

"They're so good," whispered the petite blonde girl beside her whom Poppy had introduced as Danielle.

"Delicious," agreed Jolene. Bits of dialogue fluttered around her. A story of an older brother with handsome friends, reports of new fashions in the shops, talk of the new dance craze — the black bottom — whispered wishes with boys' names attached. Jolene listened contentedly.

Suzanna tapped the table with her half-empty glass. "I have a surprise," she announced, her hazel eyes dancing. Jolene stole a glance at Poppy, who was wearing a complicit smile. "Mother knows the gentleman who owns the Laurier Palace Theatre, and he's given us six tickets to tomorrow's matinée. That's one for each of us."

"Tomorrow?" shrieked one of the girls. "Why that's for *Upstage* with Norma Shearer."

Suzanna nodded and the girls almost bounced out of their seats. Poppy leaned towards Jolene. "Do you like Norma Shearer?" she asked.

"Why wouldn't I?" replied Jolene ambiguously.

"I adore her," added one of the girls. "I've seen all her films, except *Upstage*. It's the one about the lives of the vaudeville troupe."

Jolene's curiosity was growing. Danielle shifted uncomfortably and Jolene noticed that her friendly expression had given way to obvious disappointment. "Are you all right?"

Danielle nodded. The conversation at the table waned. "It's so kind of you, Suzie," Danielle said, "but I won't be able to come."

Catching sight of Jolene's blank eyes, Danielle quickly explained. "My father has been convinced by our parish priest that movies are a bad influence on children. He also supports the idea of closing the theatres on Sundays, because it's a holy day." She tapped her milkshake glass, slightly embarrassed. "So I never get to go."

"Don't tell him," suggested Suzanna. "I'm not sure Papa knows." She shot a questioning look at Poppy who shook her head.

But Danielle's frown remained. "Papa's sure to see me in line if I try to go," she said hopelessly. She turned again towards Jolene. "My father's a fireman at the station down the street from the Laurier Palace Theatre and we'd have to line up for hours."

"No, we won't," said Suzanna, placing the purse Jolene had found earlier on the table. Reaching inside, she withdrew six tickets and distributed them to the girls. Danielle reached for hers, but did not pick it up.

"We won't have to wait in line at all, and we can leave by the back doors," said Suzanna. "It would be so much fun if you could come with us, Danielle."

Danielle fidgeted with her delicate fingers, obviously torn. Jolene wanted to console and comfort her. Danielle's anxiety remained firmly etched on her features.

"Will you join us, Jolene?" Poppy asked, her eyes bright and inviting.

Jolene considered the question. Tomorrow was Sunday

in the present as well, and as far as she knew they had no special plans. Grandma and Mom would probably spend the day getting ready for Thanksgiving dinner on Monday. "I'd really like to," she said honestly.

A loud celebratory shout followed by the clatter of cascading coins interrupted the girls' discussion. They watched a young man at the slot machines toss his hat in the air while his friends clustered about. Gradually, the girls' talk resumed in loose phrases around the table.

Danielle leaned towards Jolene. "Will your parents let you go to the cinema?"

Jolene shook her head. Grandpa would freak if she told him she'd gone back in time alone, and Mom and Dad, well, they'd think she was completely crazy. "No," she admitted, "if I come, it will be without them knowing."

The tiny blonde girl scrutinized Jolene carefully. "If you go, I'll go," she said at last.

"Okay," said Jolene, appreciating the courage she had shown. "Then I'll be there."

Danielle smiled nervously, but her eyes glowed with anticipation.

"Where is the Laurier Palace Theatre?" Jolene asked.

"On the corner of St. Catherine Street and Dézéry Street," Suzanna replied. "It's not far from here."

"Shall I meet you there at 1:30?" asked Danielle bravely.

"Sure," said Jolene smiling. It would be the first 1920s film for both of them.

Jolene reminded herself to watch for the theatre on the way home. The rest of the girls had arranged to meet upstairs on the balcony. The first person to arrive would save six seats, preferably in the front row, and the others would join them as they came in. Pocketing her ticket, Jolene felt the escalating thrill of adventure.

For another hour, Jolene sat at the table, listening, adding an occasional comment, and joining in the easy laughter. If she had lived in the past, she would have liked to have had these girls as friends.

"Did you have a boyfriend, Jolene, where you came from?" asked Poppy.

Jolene felt the colour inch up her neck. Could she count Stephan as a boyfriend? "Kind of."

The table leaned forward. Ten excited eyes studied hers.

"There's this boy I like."

"Is he handsome?" asked Suzanna.

"Very," declared Jolene, while the girls sighed with vicarious pleasure.

"Is he kind?" asked Danielle.

"Exceptionally."

"And does he know how to treat a girl?" asked Poppy.

Jolene nodded. Stephan was special, that was for certain.

"Does he like you, too?" asked Suzanna.

"I . . . I think so," said Jolene. "I hope so. It's just that he's older than me."

The girls nodded knowingly until a classmate, Gisella, strolled by, stopping to greet them. As Suzanna introduced them, Jolene saw Gisella's face drain of colour. "You're Poppy's double," she breathed and Jolene thought her voice trembled. "That's awful, just awful."

"Why?" asked Danielle. "I think it's kind of special."

Gisella reached out as if to touch Jolene, but pulled her hand away before it made contact. Jolene felt a knot in her chest begin to form. "When you meet your double, they say that means you'll die." The girls gasped and Jolene shrank back into the booth. "It happened to my uncle," continued Gisella, fear in her eyes. "He saw his look-alike one day while he was at the train station. Two days later he was killed in an accident at work." Gisella shivered involuntarily and Jolene felt the mood in the booth change.

"That's silly!" declared Suzanna, but her voice quivered.

Gisella shook her head. Jolene raised her eyes and watched Poppy, who was watching her. Immediately, she felt their bond strengthen, almost as if the two of them were one.

"I heard a story like that once," said Jolene trying to sound nonchalant, "but the lady that died was very old. I suspect she was hallucinating." Then she pinched the skin on her forearm, leaving an angry red blotch. "According to the story I heard, one of the doubles is also supposed to be a ghost." Poppy raised her arms in a spooky manner and the girls relaxed as Gisella went in search of her mother. Poppy caught Jolene's eye and gave her a broad, reassuring smile. Jolene returned it, but inside her chest the pressure continued to mount. Was she Poppy's death omen?

The topic of conversation switched to the new shingled

hair styles, and Jolene looked around the drugstore. She had promised Stephan that she would discover the date and year. Pinned to the wall behind the cash register, was a small tear-off calendar. Jolene squinted to see it. It read January 1927 and the four Sundays were the 2nd, 9th, 16th and 25th. Judging from what the girls had said earlier and the fact that they were on Christmas holidays but due to return to school soon, Jolene guessed it was Saturday, January 8th. Pleased with her deduction, she leaned back into the girls' lilting voices until it was time to go.

Danielle caught her arm as she was leaving. "So I'll see you tomorrow?" Jolene nodded. "Right," agreed Danielle. "It will be our adventure." She paused. "And don't worry about what Gisella said. She's kind, but her family's a little different."

After saying her goodbyes, Jolene pulled her watch from her coat pocket. She hadn't been able to wear it because her dress was sleeveless and it was far too modern, but now she realized that she had been absent almost two hours. The time crease was still a good fifteen minute walk away. She reached the corner of St. Catherine and Dézéry Streets and searched for the theatre. An upright oval sign above the grand entrance of a large two-storey building read *Laurier Palace*. She angled towards a wooden sign advertising today's film and was shocked to feel the hot, kinetic energy of a time crease in the recessed doorway. Quickly, she stepped out of the shadow then back into it, feeling the unmistakable energy that allowed her to time-travel. Jolene hesitated. If she went through this time crease instead of the one at the church, she wouldn't have to backtrack to get home. That might save her fifteen minutes and hours of explanations. The only problem was she had no idea what was situated at this location in the present.

Glancing again at her watch, Jolene decided to risk it. As soon as a young couple had passed her, she stepped backwards into the shadow of the theatre. She felt the air tingle and grow denser as the pressure intensified. In an instant, she was swept into darkness, gasping for breath. Just when the force on her body seemed unbearable, she was thrown free into the light of the present.

She found herself leaning against a glass door in the small recessed entrance way of an apartment building. Stepping onto the sidewalk, Jolene looked around. Next door, stairs led up to double doors with dozens of small glass windows. A large white cross had been painted above them and the stone building bore the name Bethel Evangelical Temple. Jolene scampered across the street into a small park that she recognized as the one close to Grandma Rose's house and set off at a trot. It wasn't far and it was a good thing, because her shoes were obviously not made for running. By the time she reached her grandmother's house, Jolene's feet hurt and the straps dug into her ankles. Pulling them off on the front porch, she dug the key out of her pocket and inserted it into the lock. Inside the still house, she froze and listened. Chaos meowed and Jolene jumped. He was curled up on Grandma Rose's couch. Sleepily, he yawned then proceeded to groom himself. Holding her shoes and her breath, Jolene tiptoed upstairs, willing the wooden floors not to betray her.

Grandma Rose's bedroom door was still closed at the end of the hall. Relieved, Jolene slipped into her bedroom and traded her clothes for more modern ones. It was almost four o'clock and she knew that her parents would arrive shortly. Leaving her grandmother sleeping, she went down to the kitchen to start supper.

Chapter Nine

THE NOISE AT THE dinner table was enough to drown out Chaos' most persistent pleas. Jolene stooped to pick him up and set him on her lap as her family's voices blended into a chorus of excitement. Michael, Grandpa, Mom and Dad told stories about their visit to the reserve. They had witnessed traditional dances, learned about life in an aboriginal longhouse, been invited to join the native circle gathering, and taken part in a Mohawk Thanksgiving celebration. Surprisingly, Stephan was quiet, but as soon as they had finished their meal, Jolene suggested they watch the sun crash from his balcony.

"So," she asked, sitting down beside him, "did you find out anything about your family?"

"One of the elders said she remembered my great-uncle, but not my great-grandfather. I'm guessing he didn't live on the reserve, because my great-grandmother was white and there's no record of a white woman living at Kahnawake."

Jolene felt disappointment ebb from him. "What happened to your great-uncle and his family?"

"He and his son were both killed in the Quebec Bridge collapse."

"You mean my dad's researching a disaster that claimed the lives of two of your native relatives! That's amazing."

"Not really," Stephan told her. "So many of the men working on the Quebec Bridge were from the reserve that every single family lost someone."

"Did you find out how the Mohawks became such good skywalkers?"

Stephan rubbed his calloused palms together. "In 1886, a tall bridge was built over the St. Lawrence River, close to the Kahnawake reserve," he explained. "The men grew curious and began climbing the iron girders. It seems they could walk narrow beams high in the air above the river as if they were walking down a sidewalk. The construction boss noticed and hired them for the job."

"So, were they just naturals?"

"I'm not sure, but they're very proud of their history as skywalkers. The Mohawk men quickly acquired a reputation for being brave, hardworking, capable steelworkers. Soon the calls came in and the Kahnawake men started to boom out."

"Boom out?"

"That's what they call it when they leave home to go away to work on a job." Above them, the street lamp buzzed to life. "The Mohawks helped build the Empire State Building, Madison Square Gardens, the George Washington Bridge and the World Trade Center." Stephan paused. "They were also the ones called to dismantle the buildings after 9–11, and they're now working on the new World Trade Center in New York."

"Wow!" said Jolene. "There's a lot to be said for pride."

"They typically work together as a clan," explained Stephan. "Often they sing and tell stories to make the time pass. One of the Mohawk workers even played a banjo a hundred floors up last Christmas for the men."

Jolene smiled, remembering Grandpa's story. "It's still a dangerous job."

"There's a massive steel cross in the graveyard," Stephan told her solemnly.

Jolene sat silently, watching the last remnants of the sunset. "Are you glad you went?"

"Very." Stephan looked upwards, his eyes a dark background for the first faintly reflected stars overhead. "The Kahnawake people weren't surprised to see me."

"What do you mean?"

"An elder told me, 'You have been drawn back to us and your culture. It is part of your soul.'"

Jolene watched Stephan's eyes, eyes that seemed to reveal his soul at that moment. The endless look of intrigue had been replaced by something that seemed blissful.

"You really like the Mohawk ways and beliefs, don't you?"

Stephan took his time formulating a response. "They're based on respect and harmony. I like that. It makes sense to me. I especially like the Mohawk belief about the dead," he said softly. "They believe that the ancestors do not die but merely live in another world and should be kept alive in present-day realities. Their spirits continue to be part of the Mohawks' daily lives and whenever there's a ceremony, the ancestors are the first ones called."

Jolene looked sideways at the house that had been Stephan's grandmother's for over fifty years. "I'm glad you had a good day."

"I brought you something," he announced unexpectedly. Reaching into his inner jacket pocket, he handed Jolene a gift bag. Inside, wrapped in tissue paper the colour of a robin's egg, was a small dream catcher. Its feathers were soft and strong, and delicate pieces of amber glass beaded the leather strands of the web.

"I understand them now," said Stephan. "The circle represents life and the fact that everything in the living world is connected and should be celebrated and honoured. The web relates to the creation story and the feather is that of an eagle who teaches us to combine wisdom and courage."

"It's beautiful."

"And," said Stephan, "contrary to what I'd heard, dream catchers trap both the good and the bad dreams."

"Why the bad ones?"

"The woman who made it told me that we need both — the bad ones bring us courage."

"I love it," said Jolene. "Thank you."

He smiled affectionately at her. "So, what did you do today?"

"Made pies and went for a milkshake."

"A milkshake? Where?"

"At a drugstore."

Stephan was staring at her. "In which century?" he queried, although she suspected from the tone of his voice that he already knew the answer.

"I now know," she told him proudly, "that I was there on January 8, 1927."

Stephan's eyes darkened as if a cloud had just obscured two bright stars. "Didn't your grandmother notice?"

"Grandma Rose took a long nap," explained Jolene. Following the rapid progression of her thoughts, she suddenly asked, "Stephan, does Grandma Rose ever drive anymore?"

"I don't think she's driven since that incident with the dog last summer."

"What incident?"

In a voice that flowed like maple syrup, Stephan recounted how Grandma Rose had injured a dog when it had darted out in front of her car in early July. Jolene listened intently. "She doesn't trust her reflexes anymore," he told her. "She couldn't help thinking, what if that had been a kid?" Stephan paused. "I just assumed she would have mentioned it."

Jolene shook her head. Her grandmother was in her eighties and yet, because she had always been so capable, nobody really thought of her as elderly. Nobody could deny that she was aging, not even Mom.

"What else did you discover?" asked Stephan.

"That she tires more easily."

"I meant in the past."

"Oh," Jolene said. "The twenties were a pretty fun time to live. Did you know that they actually shook milkshakes by hand?"

"Sweet!"

"Yeah. And women were actually pretty liberated."

"More liberated than you?"

She considered his question seriously. "No, but they're getting there."

"So what else did you find out?"

Jolene grinned in the twilight, wondering how much of the girl talk he'd like to hear. "That Danielle's father is against movies, that Suzanna kissed a boy named Henri at a Christmas party, that Flo's sister has ordered a bra that flattens her . . ."

"Enough!" said Stephan, slicing the air with his hands. "Too much information." He leaned towards her in the darkness and for a moment Jolene wondered if he might kiss her. But he rose instead.

"And," said Jolene getting up, "I discovered a second time crease. It's on the corner of St. Catherine Street and Dézéry Street." She stepped into the halo of light from the street lamp. "And I've been invited to the theatre tomorrow — to see *Upstage*."

"You're not going, are you?"

"The girls are so nice," replied Jolene, "kind of like my girlfriends at home."

"What's wrong with a boy friend?" asked Stephan. His choice of words jump-started Jolene's heart. Had he meant a boy friend or a boyfriend?

"Nothing," she said carefully.

"Your mom told me that we were going to eat around two o'clock tomorrow."

"Tomorrow? It's not even Thanksgiving Day."

"I think your dad wants to go to Quebec City on Monday."

Jolene's spirits fell. "Now what am I going to do?"

"Not time-travel," suggested Stephan. "It might be safer."

"Hmm," said Jolene, stroking the feathers of her dream catcher. "I'd feel bad though. I arranged to meet Danielle, one of the girls, prior to the show."

"If you don't show up, she'll go on her own."

"I doubt it," said Jolene. "She's too scared that her father will find out."

"Then maybe it's a good thing if she doesn't go." Stephan's voice reasoned with her from the darkest corner of the balcony.

"I guess," admitted Jolene, "although Gramps says we can't change history."

"Is he right?"

Jolene didn't answer. To the best of her knowledge, she couldn't, but what if Grandpa was wrong? What if Danielle wasn't supposed to be at the theatre tomorrow and her father did find out?

"Besides," said Stephan, "this whole doppelgänger business still bothers me." He moved towards her, then raised one hand and brushed a strand of hair from her cheek. "Don't go back, tomorrow, Jo."

"I won't be able to," replied Jolene. "We're having supper, remember?"

"Right." He let his fingers fall. "I'd better go. I've been invited to go kayaking early tomorrow morning with a friend, and I still have to get ready." He opened the front door. "See you tomorrow for supper."

"Sure," said Jolene, wishing that he could sit forever with her and count the stars that had exploded in the night sky. "And thanks for the dream catcher."

"You're welcome. Pleasant dreams."

Inside the house, Jolene resumed work on her family tree. With great care, she leafed through the photo albums, examining each picture, trying to identify the faces and places that paraded before her. In each pose, each smile, each expression, she hunted for a hint of Poppy. Grandma Rose brought her quilting to the dining room table, and together they perused her family's history, her grandmother's memories revealing bits and pieces of the larger puzzle. "Did your parents have many relatives in Montreal?" asked Jolene.

"My father's family came from northern Quebec," said Grandma Rose. "But I think my mother might have had roots in Montreal." Her thin lips parted in a sudden recollection. "Yes, I remember once as a teenage girl, a conversation about her between my father and a neighbour." Jolene listened carefully. "We were waiting for my brothers at a church picnic, and someone commented on the fact that Gus looked like Nora, our real mother. My father responded by saying that they were actually radically different. Gus intended to go on farming, while Nora, despite her efforts, had always been a Montreal girl at heart."

Jolene flipped the page and paused at a photo of Gus as a young man. She couldn't see the resemblance with Nora, except perhaps in the heart shape of his face.

"I asked Gus what Dad meant by that later," continued Grandma Rose, "and he told me a story about Mother that I'd forgotten until just now."

"Please," pleaded Jolene.

"Our mother," said Grandma Rose, "loved her music." The smile on Grandma's face unfurled like a pale pink ribbon being unwound from a spool. "In the twenties, jazz music became all the rage. Gus told me that Mother loved to sing and dance, but Father forbade her. The Catholic priests were very much against the music culture at the time. They felt it was immoral and disreputable."

"So I've heard," said Jolene, recalling Suzanna and Poppy's comments.

"But when Papa was out in the field, Mother would turn

on the radio and dance with the boys as she worked. Gus told me that when she moved, it was as if an orchestra was playing just for her. He remembers once watching her carry two buckets of water from the pump. She was dancing, a wild, lively dance, and by the time she got to the house, the buckets were almost empty, and she was soaked but smiling."

"Where did she learn to dance?"

"Probably in Montreal," said Grandma Rose, "before she was married." The telephone sounded loudly and she shuffled into the kitchen, leaving Jolene alone with the rest of her unposed questions.

Why had Nora married a straight-laced farmer if she loved the music and dance culture of the city? And what shocking news had she received on the afternoon of Grandma Rose's birth? Picking up her ruler and pencil, Jolene began filling in the more recent generations of her family tree as Michael and Grandpa wandered into the living room with the chess board.

"Oh dear," said Grandma Rose returning to the dining room and picking up her quilting.

"What's wrong?" asked Jolene.

"That was Mrs. Walters. She lives on the ground floor next door. Two of the ladies who are supposed to prepare the Thanksgiving Day dinner at the church hall are ill with the flu." Her wrinkled fingers played with the needle. "They need more hands, but the only problem is the dinner is scheduled for two o'clock, and we planned to have ours early, as well."

"We can eat later," said Michael, tapping the board with his pawn.

"We could, couldn't we?" said Grandma Rose.

Jolene felt a flutter inside her. If they postponed their dinner, she might be able to go to the movies with her new friends. But Stephan would be disappointed with her if she did. No, she decided, she would stay here tomorrow.

"You know, Rose, we could all help out at the church," offered Grandpa.

"Sure," agreed Jolene, "although you might not want to let Michael cook."

"I'm good in the kitchen," protested Michael. "You are serving mac and cheese, aren't you, Gram?"

They all laughed as Mom and Dad walked in the front door. Jolene noticed that the RV was parked on the street in front of Grandma Rose's.

Her grandmother peered at Jolene's parents over the rim of her glasses. "There's been a slight change in plans, Kate, for tomorrow." She resumed quilting. "We've postponed dinner until later tomorrow night."

"Why?" asked Mom, in a voice that sounded like a challenge. "I thought we were going to eat early?"

"I have to go help out at the church hall supper. Two of the ladies are ill."

The colour of Mom's eyes intensified. "Which is exactly

what you'll be if you keep doing these kinds of things," she declared. "Can't they find someone else?"

Grandma Rose's hands stopped. "No," she said evenly. "We host that dinner every year for those who are alone or have nowhere to go."

"I know," replied Mom, "but there are others who can help." Her eyes were dangerously dark, like an ominous thunderhead.

"Gramps and Michael and I are going to help out, too," interjected Jolene.

"What about our Thanksgiving dinner?"

"I'm sure you and I can handle it," said Dad, putting an arm around Mom's shoulders. She shook it off.

"That's not the point." There was no avoiding the storm brewing in Mom's eyes. Jolene braced herself. "It's Thanksgiving, and we should be thankful that we're here as a family."

She sounded, thought Jolene, as if she had borrowed her lines from Grandma Rose's script.

"I am," declared Grandma Rose, rising unsteadily to her feet. "But I'm also thankful for those at the church who host these meals." Before Mom could protest, she continued. "If you hadn't come this year, Kate, I may well have gone to that dinner myself." Her voice broke as she left the room.

So did Mom's expression of anger. Dad fidgeted with his keys, Michael and Grandpa's game went unnoticed. Jolene sat stunned by the realization that had just hit all of them.

"She has lots of friends," said Mom weakly.

"In the past year," said Grandpa, "she's lost three of her closest friends, including Stephan's grandma." He let his words sink in.

"I'm sure Mirette and Tom would have invited her had they been home," said Dad.

Mom's desperate expression remained.

Jolene took a deep breath. There was no time like the present. "She's old, Mom. Older than you like to think of her. Stephan told me that last summer she hit a dog with the car. She doesn't drive anymore because she's afraid her reflexes will be too slow if a child runs out in front of her." Dad moved closer to Mom as Jolene continued. "Did you know that she takes a nap most days?"

"She told me that she'd like a computer but she thinks she's too old to learn to use it," added Michael.

Still Mom did not comment.

"Age sneaks up on people," said Grandpa. "All of a sudden the things you once took for granted are challenges. And it's hard when you lose good friends. It makes you think of your own mortality more." He sighed. "And, Rose has been on a fixed income for a long time, but prices haven't stayed fixed."

Mom squared her shoulders. "If she needed help," she said, "she'd tell us."

Grandpa looked skeptical. "Pride is a mixed blessing."

Dad cleared his throat. "We'll do supper tomorrow for

six o'clock," he announced in a decisive voice. "You three go help with the meal at the church."

Nodding, Mom made her way upstairs. Jolene thought she looked like a little girl dragging her small, tired legs up massive steps.

Chapter Ten

JOLENE HEARD STEPHAN on his balcony early the next morning. She rose quickly, intending to say goodbye from her partially open window, but as she pushed the mint-coloured drapes aside, she noticed that a small black car had pulled up in front of his house. A tall girl with beautiful wavy hair stepped out of the passenger door, causing Jolene to retreat behind the drapes. "Hi Stephan," the visitor called up, waving excitedly.

"Hey Sarah," Jolene heard him call down. "I'll be there in a minute."

Jolene stepped away from the window. She had assumed that Stephan's kayaking friend would be male. He'd never mentioned Sarah before. Stephan's footsteps descended the metal staircase and Jolene looked back out the window. Sarah leaned against the car waiting, a broad smile on her suntanned face.

A sharp knock sounded on her grandmother's front door, but Jolene did not move. She heard Grandma Rose in the front entrance and then Stephan's muffled voice. His visit was brief. In minutes, he had joined Sarah, who climbed into the back seat so they could sit together. Stephan slid in next to her and the car sped away, leaving Jolene alone with her disconcerting thoughts.

Michael, Grandpa and Grandma Rose were waiting for her in the front hallway by the time she came downstairs. It had taken her longer than usual to get ready and she had skipped breakfast, too preoccupied to eat. Why hadn't Stephan told her about Sarah? Was she his girlfriend? Just a friend? The girl he'd imagined taking to a school dance?

Jolene had made a conscious effort to leave those questions locked securely in her bedroom. There was no sense spending the day brooding, especially when she could have her own fun. With that in mind, she had dressed in her jean skirt, blouse and flats, before pulling on the wrap coat she had retrieved from Grandma's attic. She might disappoint Stephan if she returned to 1927, but then he'd disappointed her as well.

"Where did you get that coat?" asked Michael when she joined them.

"It's a hand-me-down," said Jolene, winking at Grandma.

They set off for the church, walking briskly through the cool morning. Tiny transparent drops of rain clung to the grasses making them shimmer in the sunlight. A few hearty burgundy-petalled petunias stood staunchly in flower boxes around the neighbourhood. The fall frost had bypassed them, but the wind had plucked more leaves from the maple and oak trees, dropping them haphazardly on lawns and in the gutters.

They entered the hall kitchen by a side door, the clang of utensils and the sizzle of butter on the stove greeting them. After some quick introductions, they were all put to work. Three enormous bags of carrots stood waiting for Jolene. Michael began unloading stacks of plates from a cart, and Grandpa was persuaded to stir a cream sauce on the stove. Grandma Rose dived into the refrigerator and emerged with a head of lettuce in each hand, speaking in French, then English, then a combination of both. The aroma of roasting turkey, freshly baked buns and sweet cranberries wafted through the air. As soon as a bunch of carrots were peeled, they were whisked away from Jolene to be furiously chopped on cutting boards. Steam rose continually from dozens of stainless steel pots as the women called to each other, their hands and lips in constant motion.

As Jolene's hands found the rhythm of peeling, her mind drifted. Somewhere in the sunshine beyond the window, Stephan was kayaking, propelling his boat through the water as a First Nations scout might have done years ago. Jolene imagined his black hair gleaming in the sunlight, his powerful arms paddling through the rippled water, and his eyes drinking in every movement along the shoreline. It was a lovely image, except that Sarah's kayak kept drifting into the picture, her long auburn hair sparkling like burnt gold. Jolene concentrated instead on the conversation in the kitchen. The room had fallen silent, except for Grandpa's voice and an occasional soft murmur. Jolene smiled. He was telling a story, transporting every woman in the room to an earlier time, a time softened and intensified by memory.

Jolene's hands were stained orange by the time the carrots were done. Michael had managed to set seventy-five places with all the knives on the wrong side, and Grandpa's story had ended in the usual high-spirited laughter. Grandma Rose was carving radishes to adorn the salad. She was seated beside her neighbor, Mrs. Walters, who was telling her about her niece moving to Montreal. "She's been away at school, and now she has a job here. If we had room for her, we'd take her in, but we're bursting at the seams already."

Jolene joined the dish brigade, drying until her tea towel was sopping wet. The turkeys were browning, the gravy was underway and the smells in the kitchen made Jolene's stomach growl. Michael was perched on a ladder, hanging Thanksgiving decorations. Jolene wiped her brow. It was 1:25 and they were basically done.

She sat down at the table opposite her grandmother. "If

you don't need me any longer, Gram, maybe I'll go," she suggested, wondering if she had time to reach the theatre. "There's something I'd like to do before supper."

Grandma Rose's frosted curls bobbed. "Off you go, Jolene. And thank you for all your help."

"You're welcome," said Jolene, leaping to her feet. Grabbing her coat, she slipped out the door without letting Michael or Grandpa know she was leaving. Grandma Rose would tell them later, and by that time she would be years away. Zipping around the church, she passed quickly through the time crease into Montreal in the 1920s. Her flats were easier to run in than her heeled shoes and soon she was sprinting down Dézéry Street towards the queue at the Laurier Palace Theatre. Jolene hesitated. Stephan had promised to look into the time crease at the theatre, but she hadn't seen him this morning. He would have told her if there was reason for concern. Or maybe he'd been too anxious to see Sarah to remember his promise.

Clutching the ticket in her pocket, Jolene looked around the intersection. Movie-goers crowded the street, but she couldn't see Danielle anywhere. "Jolene," said a girl's voice beside her, and Jolene turned to see Danielle, her coat collar pulled up over her chin and her hat pulled down. "I didn't think you were coming," said the blonde girl, but Jolene could hear the relief in her voice.

"I said I would," said Jolene. "I had to finish some chores first." They bypassed the lineup, pushed their way into the lobby, handed their tickets to an usher and asked directions to the balcony. The stairwell, which was located at the front of the lobby, was dim and divided into three sections, which turned and twisted at every landing. When they finally reached the top of the staircase, Jolene pushed the door open, emerging onto the balcony followed closely by Danielle. The lights were still up, but the seats were packed and there were even children and a few adults standing at the back near the glass projection booth. Quickly they walked towards the front row of the balcony. Jolene caught sight of Poppy, and she and Danielle joined the girls, Jolene sliding into the plush chair next to the aisle.

Below her, a screen that looked too small for the building hung on the front wall. Spectators occupied the hundreds of chairs on the main floor below. Jolene estimated the seating to be close to a thousand, and there was definitely a full house. The audience was almost entirely made up of children, ranging in age from no more than four, all the way to teenagers of fifteen or sixteen, with only a few adults amongst them.

"Everybody's here," squeaked Suzanna. "All our schoolmates and neighbours."

Poppy's green eyes sparkled and her gestures were animated. But next to her, Danielle slumped in her chair. Any of these people, Jolene realized, could tell Danielle's father. She felt a pang of guilt. A nagging voice that sounded like a blend of Grandpa's and Stephan's echoed in her ears.

The lights began to drop. A young boy perched on an older girl's lap behind Jolene kicked the back of her seat, and the girl warned him that he could only sit there if he didn't squirm. Two young girls no older than five had squeezed into a seat together across the aisle from Jolene.

With so many bodies in the theatre, Jolene began to perspire. She unfastened the button of her coat and unwrapped it slightly, careful not to reveal her modern-day attire. Danielle, too, had adjusted her coat and relaxed into her chair. The theatre was now blanketed in darkness. An excited murmur swept through the crowd.

Light illuminated the screen and the buzz of the theatre increased. Numbers flickered and Jolene waited for the sound to begin. The words *Get 'Em Young* flashed and Jolene turned towards Danielle, suddenly confused. "I thought we were watching *Upstage*."

"We are," whispered Poppy from the seat beside Danielle. "This is just a short comedy."

Piano music blared but not from the film. A light in the orchestra below the screen stage revealed a pianist at the keyboard. The actors' and actresses' mouths produced no sound. Instead, subtitles played beneath their images. "It's a silent film," whispered Jolene amazed.

Danielle giggled beside her. "What were you expecting? That the actors would talk?"

Jolene grinned to herself. She settled back into her seat to watch her first 1920s comedy, soon dissolving into laughter along with the other girls. But about ten minutes into the show, an uneasy feeling enveloped her, along with the faint but unmistakable smell of smoke. She turned her head towards the projection booth, but could see only the steady circle of light from the projector diffusing into the theatre. None of the other girls seemed to have noticed the smoke, but dark, fiery thoughts plagued Jolene. Time creases existed for a reason. She glanced at Poppy who was absorbed in the film. Doppelgängers signalled death. Was she Poppy's death omen? "Do you smell smoke?" she whispered across Danielle to her double.

"It's probably just someone having a cigarette," Poppy whispered back.

But Jolene felt Danielle's body grow tense and rigid between them. She leaned over the balcony railing as the crowd roared with laughter at the antics on the screen. There was no haze over the main floor, but a definite pall of smoke had begun to form in the midsection of the balcony. Two children half-stood, pointing at the floor.

Jolene gripped Danielle's hand, her heartbeat edging upwards. She leaned towards the others. "We have to get out of here."

"Why?" asked Suzanna.

"Can't you smell the smoke?"

At least a dozen children had risen from their balcony seats, their slender fingers fanning the air in front of them. A thin, but discernible column of smoke rose from the floor.

Jolene and Danielle were on their feet when two ushers appeared in the aisle carrying fire extinguishers. "It's nothing," they called as the children in the midsection rows let them by. "Just a little smoke." Their voices were confident and strong. "Stay seated. It's nothing."

"Don't worry," said Suzanna motioning for Jolene and Danielle to sit back down. "It's under control."

But Jolene knew she was wrong. Nothing was under control. And if there was a fire in this crowded theatre . . . "Poppy," she said, "let's go. Now!"

Poppy's eyes — so much like her own — met hers. Suzanna put a hand to her lips to shush Jolene. Danielle's fear was as tangible as her own, but the other girls remained engrossed in the film.

On their right, an usher arrived with an axe and started breaking apart the floorboards. "Let's go!" pleaded Jolene. Most of the audience was standing despite the fact that the film continued to play. Suzanna and Poppy perched on the edge of their seats. "Come on," urged Jolene, but the girls still hesitated. Turning, Jolene started up the stairs. If they saw she was serious about leaving, maybe they would follow her. Fiery flames leaped from the floorboards into the theatre, unleashing a sudden panic. Children scrambled from their seats, screaming, "*Au feu! Au feu!* Fire!"

The passage to the balcony doors was suddenly filled with people. Jolene tried to push her way through, but the spectators who had been seated in the rows behind her now blocked the aisle. Running and shoving, fear-filled children swarmed the doors, flung them open and forced their way into the dark stairwell. Jolene looked back over her shoulder and caught sight of Danielle's blonde curls. Where were the others? Grabbing Danielle's hand, Jolene pressed forward. They were bumped and jostled. Danielle fell and Jolene reached down to pull her upright as the heels of shoes dug into them. A feverish urgency filled the theatre.

They were still a few metres from the stairwell entrance and the smoke was now thick and acrid. Pulling her collar up over her mouth, Jolene urged herself to stay calm in the growing madness. But the panic in the mob was spreading. Someone grabbed her hair, pulling her backwards, and a boy, standing on the back of the last row of chairs, leaped over Danielle, his shoe striking her nose. She stumbled, bleeding now from her face, but regained her balance as the crowd surged forward. Desperate cries filled the theatre and abruptly the lights came on. Jolene could see the entrance to the stairwell now, filled with flailing limbs and jammed with bodies. Cries, shrieks, and anxious, muffled protests arose from the narrow passage, eliciting a vision of bodies heaped on the twisting landings. Jolene made a sudden, decisive decision as a fire alarm blared outside.

"This way," she cried, turning away from the exit and jerking Danielle's arm.

Danielle turned to follow Jolene as she scrambled over a row of chairs to avoid the crowd. "Where are we going?" she called. Jolene coughed, conscious of a burning sensation in her throat and eyes. No flames were visible, but the smoke had obscured almost everything. The aisle on the other side was congested and impassable. Shrieks and screams rose and Jolene felt the panic in the balcony sweep through her. If they made it back to the first row, could they jump? She tried to remember how far it was from the railing to the main floor. Beside her Danielle swooned and she reached out to steady the girl. "Cover your mouth," Jolene instructed, but she, too, felt faint and nauseous. Smoke seared her eyes and parched her mouth. Her stomach heaved.

Suddenly, she felt a man's hand on her shoulder. Turning, she saw a theatre employee, his mouth covered with a handkerchief. He motioned for the girls to follow him, and they did so, staggering past the projection booth towards the far stairwell with a small group of children. Moans and groans, plaintive desperate pleas came from the passageway. They'd never get past the jam of bodies inside. But the man stopped before they reached the stairwell and, in the dim light, Jolene could see that they were adjacent to a small window. Prying the window open, the man motioned for them to climb through it, then stooped to pick up a young, semi-conscious boy who lay draped across a seat. Jolene pushed Danielle towards the open window. Barely conscious, the tiny blonde girl half-squeezed, half-fell through the opening. Quickly, Jolene followed her out onto the wooden marquee that jutted out over the sidewalk on St. Catherine Street. Fresh air hit her face and she gulped eagerly. Firefighters had constructed a rope ladder and were helping the children down it.

Jolene crouched beside Danielle, feeling weak and dizzy. Desperately, she tried to revive her friend who had all but collapsed into a state of unconsciousness. The triangular peaked hat of a firefighter came into view and Danielle coughed weakly. "Danielle!" The man's eyes were wide, his pupils as bright as the brass buttons on his uniform. "It's my daughter!" he called down to his colleague. Quickly, he collected Danielle's listless body and carried her down the ladder. Another firefighter arrived to help Jolene. As she descended, she searched for Danielle and her father, but they were lost in the crowd.

With the aid of a policeman, Jolene traversed the street, which was full of anxious spectators. Hands supported her, lifted her, set her gently down on a wooden crate. Voices consoled her. Jolene abandoned herself to the helping hands and comforting tones and surrendered to her tears.

Alarms filled the winter air and a fire truck arrived to join the others that were already there. Firefighters rushed into the building or to aid their colleagues who were in the process of axing a hole in the wall of the theatre. Jolene knew from the location that the hole would lead directly into the east stairwell. She shuddered to think what they might find. Screams burst from the smoking building, only to be drowned out by the clanging of ambulance bells and the blaring of sirens. Someone offered her a handkerchief and Jolene wiped the soot and smoke from her face. Beside her, a woman wailed in the street and a child sobbed piteously.

Jolene tried to watch the entrance to the theatre and the dwindling stream of crying, distraught children that emerged from it. But there were too many people and too much confusion to keep track of those who stumbled into the street. Silently, she prayed that Poppy and Suzanna had survived. But there was no ignoring the reality that surrounded her. Had she been the omen of Poppy's death? "No," whispered Jolene, choked with emotion, but the word held no power to convince her.

When no more children stumbled from the theatre doors, the crowd waited. The firefighters had gained entrance via the marquee and the water from their hoses dripped from the second floor. Every few minutes, a firefighter would emerge, carrying a child clinging to life or one who had succumbed to death. Jolene watched as a lone firefighter staggered from the doorway, his face convulsing with bitter sobs. She turned away. She could no longer bear to watch. No longer bear to think. No longer bear to feel.

"Jo!"

Jolene's chin jerked upwards. That was Michael's voice. She'd recognize it anywhere. But why would Michael be here? Without warning, her brother and grandfather were beside her, their arms around her.

"Are you all right?" asked Michael, releasing her from his smothering grip.

A nurse with two black smudges of ash on her right cheek was speaking to her grandfather. She helped Jolene to her feet then handed her over to Grandpa, who cradled her head against his chest. "Let's go," he said. "Let's take you home."

The air on Dézéry Street revived her and Jolene realized that Michael and her grandfather must have come through the time crease at the church. The one in front of the theatre had been hacked to pieces by the firefighters. With one last look backward and with tears streaming down her smoke-blackened face, Jolene let herself be led away from the tragedy.

"Stephan arrived just after you left," said Michael. "He went crazy when he discovered that you weren't at home or at the church, especially when Grandma Rose admitted that she'd forgotten to give you his note."

"His note?" asked Jolene.

"Apparently, he left a note for you this morning about the fire," explained Grandpa. "But Rose forgot about it."

So he had discovered something, and he had tried to warn her before he left with Sarah.

"When we told him you were gone, he was frantic," said Grandpa. "He told Michael everything and Michael had the good sense to tell me."

"Seventy-six children died," added Michael, "mostly from smoke inhalation. Some were trampled in the stairwell."

Fresh tears came in rivers for Jolene.

Michael put an arm around his sister's shoulders. "Stephan said you had some friends in the theatre. I'm sorry, Jo."

The church was now in sight. "Where is Stephan?" Jolene asked.

"I sent him back to the hall to tell Rose not to wait for us," said Grandpa. "I'm not sure if he'll be there or at home."

Jolene trudged on, coughing and wheezing. "Why is there a time crease at the church?" she asked, as the steeple came into view.

"It's where the funeral for most of the children took place," said Grandpa. "Jo, I can't begin to tell you . . ." His voice died, but Jolene could see the lines of anger between the creases of concern on his face.

"I'm sorry, Gramps," she said, and she truly was.

"We'll talk more later."

They had reached the church. Michael leaned nonchalantly against the stone walls as a family pushing an old-fashioned stroller passed them. They stared at Michael's wind breaker and jeans before hurrying onwards. As soon as they had gone, Michael jumped into the crease. Grandpa held Jolene's hand firmly and the next thing she knew, she was being hurled through time. She lurched forward into the sunshine of the twenty-first century, arriving at Stephan's side.

"Jo!" He grabbed her in a hug, lifting her completely off the ground and crushing her against him. "You're okay." He let her go. "I couldn't believe it when . . ." He let out a deep breath. "I'm guessing you know the story."

Jolene nodded. Words failed her.

"I'm so glad you're safe."

Jolene took a deep breath. "Did all the girls die?" she whispered.

"I don't know, Jo," Stephan said honestly. "We'll have to look at the Archives."

The sound of dishes being cleared and grateful conversation escaped out the church hall's doors. More than seventy men and women with nowhere else to go had just enjoyed a delicious Thanksgiving dinner.

Together they headed towards Grandma Rose's place. Jolene's tears had finally ceased, but she could not block out the horrific images that came unbidden or the terrifying shrieks that sounded within her head.

"It's such a tragedy," said Grandpa, putting his arm around her.

"The children panicked," said Jolene. "It was awful."

"According to the reports I read," said Stephan, "some of them jumped from the balcony to the ground floor. Others tried to escape down the twisting stairwells, but they created a bottleneck. Twelve children were trampled to death. The rest died of asphyxiation. When the firefighters arrived, it looked like a dormitory of sleeping children."

Had Poppy been one of those sleeping children? Jolene crunched a brittle leaf beneath her shoe and followed Stephan into his home. Grandpa had suggested that she shower at his place to avoid having to explain her smoky state to Mom or Dad. Michael would bring a change of clothes over as soon as he could.

"I should have given you the note myself," said Stephan, switching on a lamp.

"Grandma Rose forgot," said Jolene. "It wasn't your fault."

"She didn't tell me that you'd postponed dinner either," said Stephan. "Maybe she thought it wouldn't matter."

Or maybe her grandmother's memory was failing with age, thought Jolene.

Stephan went to fetch a clean towel while Jolene waited in the living room. She stood, exhausted, but reluctant to sit on the clean furniture. "Did you have a nice time kayaking?" she called after him.

"The paddling was great today," replied Stephan. "And," he added excitedly, "when we stopped for lunch, an eagle alighted on a branch above me." He returned to the room with a towel. "Remember how your grandfather was telling us about the Mohawks seeing an animal in a significant way four times and that animal becoming an animal spirit?" Jolene nodded. "Well, I found the eagle on the family tree, and then there was the one that followed me while I was cycling, and today's eagle makes three."

Jolene couldn't resist his contagious smile. "You might have to go kayaking more often."

"Maybe," said Stephan, staring down at the coffee table.

Jolene's eyes followed his gaze. On the table was a close-up photo of Stephan and Sarah, their heads together, smiling brightly. "Sarah thinks I should join her kayaking club next year," he said. "I'm thinking about it."

A sickly feeling took hold of Jolene, like an invisible poison seeping through her body. She wondered how many times a week Stephan would train beside Sarah as she turned her admiring eyes on him and let her beautiful hair fall loose over her shoulders. "It sounds ideal," she said bitterly. "And at least you'd know someone to start with." Jealousy, anger, sorrow and revenge filled her.

Stephan looked from the photo to her, his mouth set in a firm line. "Why is it," he asked handing her the towel, "that there's a good side and a bad side to everything?"

"There's a bad side?" asked Jolene, wrestling with emotions that threatened to overwhelm her.

Stephan let out a long, heartfelt sigh. "It's hard," he said gently, "when a girl likes you and you like someone else." He looked straight at Jolene. "It's really hard to know how to tell her, especially if you've been friends for a while."

Jolene felt as if she'd been slapped across the face. Resentment flared like an angry flame, only to be doused by humiliation. She looked away so Stephan could not see the tears that threatened to fall, and fought the urge to sprint from the room, away from him, away from photos of Sarah, away from the jealousy and humiliation that choked her from the inside out. Why had he been frantic with worry?

Why had he hugged her tightly after she'd returned from the fire? She banished that last image from her mind, erecting a mental barricade against all the others that flooded her thoughts. All this time he'd been so kind and considerate. He'd helped her with her family tree, researched disasters, bought her a dream catcher. But she wasn't the one he liked. She was the friend who had showered him with unwanted affection.

"Where's the bathroom?" she asked, pasting an artificial smile on her lips. Stephan motioned down the hallway and she went in that direction. It was the longest hallway of her life.

Chapter Eleven

UPSTAIRS AT GRANDMA ROSE'S, Jolene stretched out on her bed. Had she been Poppy's doppelgänger? Had she been the harbinger of death? Jolene tried to order her thoughts. If Poppy had died in the fire, then her name would be among those killed at the theatre. After Thanksgiving, she would visit the Archives. Until then . . . Jolene pulled the dream catcher from the lamp and gave in to the fatigue that consumed her.

A faint but persistent knock roused her from a heavy, dreamless sleep. Michael nudged her bedroom door open and stepped inside. "Dinner's almost ready. How are you feeling?"

Jolene sat up, rubbing a kink in her neck. "Okay, I guess."

Her brother plunked down on the bed next to her. "You're such an idiot, Jo!"

"Gee thanks."

He traced the squares of the quilt. "No, really. Do you know how easily you could have been killed?"

Jolene had tried not to think about that. "I know," she admitted now. "It was stupid."

"*Très* stupid!" said Michael, but his face betrayed a deep affection and concern for her. "Didn't it ever occur to you to check out the time period or the area around the time creases?"

"Yes, and Stephan and I did look into the one at the church before we knew what year it was."

"And the one at the theatre?"

"I didn't get Stephan's note and, well, I'd promised him I wouldn't go back again except . . ."

"Except?"

"Except I really miss my girlfriends, Michael. It's hard being away, and Poppy and the girls were so kind and fun. I didn't think it would be such a big deal to go see a movie with them."

"Yeah, well you were wrong," said Michael curtly. He rose impatiently. "Why'd you go back alone?"

Jolene shrugged. "Stephan can't time-travel. What choice did I have?"

"Uh, you have a brother who can!"

Jolene closed her eyes against Michael's accusing stare. "I'm sorry, Michael. I never thought . . ." She had excluded him, shared their secret, shut him out. Michael set her hairbrush down on the dresser with a bang and Jolene felt a sharp pang of remorse. "I'm sorry, Michael, really."

Her brother's gaze softened. "Never mind," he told her. "Save it for Gramps. You're gonna need it." Jolene cringed and Michael peered out her half-open door as Grandma Rose passed in the hallway.

"We'd better go down for dinner," said Jolene, swinging her legs over the edge of the bed.

"Yeah." Michael paused and Jolene heard her grandmother's footsteps in the front entrance. "By the way, things aren't so good between Mom and Grandma Rose."

"What happened?"

"When Gram got home from the church, Mom presented her with a cheque." Jolene held her breath and Michael continued. "I guess Grandma Rose ripped it into tiny pieces and locked herself in her bedroom."

"Great!" said Jolene, falling into step beside her brother. "Dinner ought to be a blast."

Downstairs, Mom hovered over the table, a casserole of sweet potatoes covered with brown sugar and pecans in one oven-mitted hand. Jolene sat between Grandpa and Michael, opposite Grandma Rose and Stephan. Dinner, consisting of turkey, stuffing, mashed potatoes, sweet potato, salad, gingered carrots and cranberries looked scrumptious. Sparkling non-alcoholic cider filled the children's glasses while

Dad uncorked a bottle of white wine. But Jolene hardly noticed the mouth-watering aromas or delicious food. Instead, she felt only the undeniable tension between her mother and grandmother.

Jolene studied Grandma Rose's eyes. They were sunken and red, and she was certain that she was not the only one who had cried a river today. Mom, too, looked frazzled and flustered, and Dad seemed to be strung as taut as a guy wire. Only Stephan, who arrived just before dinner was served, seemed somewhat relaxed.

"To Thanksgiving and family," he said, raising his glass of cider. "And thank you for inviting me."

All around the table, hands reached for wine glasses. Jolene clinked Grandpa's glass gently and watched as Mom's and Grandma's glasses met in a quiet crash. Dishes circulated and Jolene filled her plate, but without her usual zeal for Thanksgiving dinner.

"So Stephan," said Dad, "how was your kayaking?"

"Great!" Stephan ladled cranberries onto his turkey. "And I heard from your professor friend today."

"Already! Did he have any genealogical information for you?"

Jolene listened with interest. The professor who had taken them to the reserve had promised Stephan that he would look into his lineage.

"He discovered that three other members of my family were also killed in the Quebec Bridge collapse."

"You lost five family members in that disaster!" exclaimed

Dad. "It was a true tragedy, and probably completely avoidable."

Dad's words struck a chord with Jolene. Had the deaths she witnessed today also been avoidable? She had seen the fatal panic that had swept through the theatre. An employee had managed to save some children, including herself. Perhaps if someone else had stayed to organize the evacuation, more would have been saved. Beside her, Michael ate ravenously while Jolene poked at her food. She glanced across the table at Stephan, but looked rapidly away as he caught her eye. In an effort to avoid reliving his painful words, she focused on her father's.

Dad was explaining how the tragedy at the bridge could have been prevented. "When the Quebec Bridge Company decided to build a bridge that would span the St. Lawrence River in the early 1900s, they faced a serious challenge. It would be the largest cantilever bridge in the world at that time, and not only did it have to carry trains, streetcars and wagons, but it also had to leave the middle of the river clear for steamers to pass through to the Atlantic. Theodore Cooper, a renowned bridge builder, was hired as the supervising consultant, even though his ill health meant that he would not actually be on-site but in New York. He was sixty years old at the time, but he was keen to work on this bridge, which he considered the pinnacle of his career as an engineer." Dad poured gravy over a small mountain of potatoes. "Early on, plans were drawn up by the Phoenix Bridge

Company in New York and approved by Cooper, based on the engineer's estimates. But by the time the actual working plans were completed in 1905, they discovered that the actual weight of the cantilever was heavier than they'd estimated — eight million pounds heavier."

"Back to the drawing board," quipped Michael, shovelling stuffing into his mouth.

"It should have been," said Dad, "but the Prince of Wales was coming."

"Huh?" said Mom. "What does a prince have to do with a bridge?"

"The federal government, who was helping fund the bridge, wanted it finished prior to the Prince's visit in 1908, so he could officially open it to celebrate the province's three hundredth anniversary."

"The things princes have to do," observed Michael.

"Construction of the bridge had already begun when Cooper saw the final drawings."

"What did he do?" asked Stephan.

"He was torn. He didn't want to waste time ripping down the portion of the bridge that had already been constructed, but eight million pounds was a big differential. In the end, he convinced himself that even with the additional load, there was a sufficient safety margin."

"He was wrong," said Grandpa dryly.

"In June," continued Dad, "an on-site engineer, Norman McClure, reported that two chords, the outside horizontal pieces running the length of the bridge, were slightly out of alignment. Cooper seemed undisturbed by the news, and in July they started to build the central suspended span, which just put more stress on the chords. Then in August, McClure reported that the chords appeared bent. Cooper was troubled but couldn't explain why the bending had occurred. An on-site inspector, however, noted that the bends were increasing."

"Didn't they stop construction?" asked Mom.

"No. On August 27th, two days prior to the collapse, the inspector noticed that the chords were now more than two inches out of alignment and unmistakably bent. He reported this to McClure who sent a letter to Cooper. Then McClure went to New York himself to see Cooper on the morning of August 29th." Dad glanced around the table; all eyes watched him. "In the meantime, the men continued to work."

Grandma Rose shook her head, a sombre expression on her face. "Weren't they afraid?"

"I imagine so," said Dad, "but they trusted the engineers." He dabbed his lips with a napkin and continued. "After speaking to McClure, Cooper decided not to add any more load to the bridge."

"Was it too late?" asked Jolene.

"No."

Jolene's eyes narrowed with confusion. So too, she noticed, had Michael's.

"Instead of contacting the worksite directly, Cooper thought it best to go through the Phoenix Bridge Company in New York, so he sent them a telegram advising them to . . ." Dad's fingers formed quotation marks in the air. "Add no more load to bridge till after due consideration of facts."

"That's pretty ambiguous," declared Mom.

"He also mentioned in his telegram that McClure would arrive at the Phoenix Bridge Company's office by five that evening." Dad sipped his wine. "When the engineer at Phoenix got the message, he decided not to notify the workers in Quebec until after the meeting."

Jolene let out a sad sigh. How could so many small decisions have such a dramatic effect on so many people's lives?

"McClure arrived at five with news from Quebec that the engineers on-site were sending a report to the Phoenix Bridge Company the next morning."

"Oh no," said Jolene, already anticipating another delay in stopping work on the bridge.

"They reached the decision to do nothing just after 5:30, almost the exact moment the bridge fell."

"What a shame!" said Grandma Rose. "If someone had just had the sense to take action instead of waiting."

Mom nodded, and Jolene couldn't help thinking how alike she and Grandma Rose looked at that moment, lost in thought, touched by the tragic story of a preventable disaster. Grandma Rose's words echoed inside Jolene's head. Jolene stared at her plate. She had witnessed a preventable tragedy earlier that day, Dad had just told them about another one, and now she was watching a much smaller tragedy unfold right here in Grandma Rose's house. And yet nobody had had the sense to take action. Instead, they had all waited for Grandma and Mom to reach a resolution. Jolene took a deep breath. "I wonder if you're like any of your relatives who were killed that day, Stephan?" she asked.

Stephan shrugged.

"We all inherit traits from our ancestors," Jolene continued, "although I can't decide if I'm more like Mom or Grandma."

"In what way?" asked Dad.

"Well," said Jolene summoning her courage, "when I feel guilty about something, I often get angry just like Mom does." Dad shot her a warning look, but Jolene replied with a reassuring smile. "And when I'm scared or need help, I'm often too proud to ask, just like Grandma." The table fell silent.

"Jolene," said Dad sternly, "this is neither the time nor place."

"But it is," insisted Jolene. "It's Thanksgiving and I'm grateful that I'm descended from my mother and grandmother, because they're both strong, caring, talented, and — "

"— Incredibly stubborn people," finished Michael. Grandpa smiled beneath his moustache.

"That's enough!" Dad's voice rose.

"They have a point," said Grandpa. He inclined his head

towards Grandma Rose. "Rose, I greatly admire your strength — the way you've maintained this house and continued your life alone for so many years. I know from experience that's not easy. And I also know what it's like to grow old and start to question your memory, your abilities, your willpower and strength."

Jolene saw her grandmother nod, almost imperceptibly.

"And Kate," said Grandpa. "How you manage a family, work fulltime, do research and accommodate graduate students, always amazes me."

Mom's face still wore a troubled expression, but she acknowledged Grandpa's words with a slight inclination of her chin. The room had gone deathly quiet.

"To err is human," quoted Jolene gently.

"And to forgive is divine," concluded Stephan.

Mom and Grandma both had their heads bowed, their eyes downcast. Hope rested silently on Jolene's shoulders.

Finally, Mom pushed her chair back and stood up, her almost-empty plate in her hand. Jolene closed her eyes and willed her mother to say something apologetic. "I think I'll get the pies," Mom announced.

Jolene felt her heart plunge. She chided herself for being so stupid. How could she be so naïve to think that her comments would help end an argument that had endured for so many years?

Mom stopped and turned back to the table. "Would you like to help, Mom?" she asked.

Grandma Rose adjusted her glasses as if contemplating the question, and then rose to her feet. "It would be a pleasure," she replied with a genuine smile.

As soon as they had disappeared into the kitchen, all eyes at the table turned to Jolene. "What?" she said defensively. "I got tired of waiting."

Dad laughed. "From whom did you inherit your impatience?" he asked.

Chapter Twelve

DAD WAS IN A hurry to leave the next day. "Let's go," he called. "I want to beat at least some of the holiday traffic."

Yawning, Jolene set her backpack down and slid her feet into her runners. It had been late last night when she had finally fallen asleep to the sound of Mom's and Grandma's heated discussion. But at least they had talked, and this morning over breakfast Dad had informed the twins that Mom had decided to stay with Grandma Rose while they went to Quebec City. That was a good thing and a bad thing — first, it meant that they were both willing to try and resolve things, but it also meant that there would be room for Stephan to join them on their trip. How she was supposed to deal with that constant reminder of rejection was too overwhelming to think about.

Jolene grabbed her jacket, picked Chaos up in a squeeze, and then turned to say goodbye to Mom and Grandma. She gave each of them an extra long hug before leaving them standing side by side in the doorway.

Mom and Grandma had not been the only ones to have a serious discussion last night. Grandpa had severely reprimanded her for time-travelling on her own. Going back alone hadn't been safe and travelling without having explored the time period had also been a mistake. As she had listened to Grandpa, Jolene had tried not to think of the possible consequences of her actions. But fiery nightmares had haunted her last night.

Now in the RV, those fiery nightmares had been replaced by the difficult reality of having Stephan seated beside her. A day ago, she would have been thrilled by the knowledge that he was going to be with her when they visited the Quebec Bridge site and the old city of Quebec. She would have been delighted to have his company as Dad took photos of the bridge to complete the research he had done in Montreal. And it would have been a privilege to walk next to him as they retraced the steps of the early explorers who had first encountered the Mohawk people. But all that had changed. Taking out her novel, Jolene chose to escape.

She had almost finished her book three hours later, when Dad brought the RV to a halt on the south side of the Quebec Bridge. One by one, they stepped out into an autumn postcard. Two enormous rectangular towers rose above the bridge near either end. The arms of the bridge were anchored to the shore on either side while the cantilevers, which projected out over the river, resembled horizontal diamond-shaped laceworks of steel. These were supported by foundation piers beneath the towers. But the cantilevers did not meet in the middle. Instead, a centrally suspended bridge spanned the distance between them. Jolene knew that cantilever bridges worked on the principle that forces were distributed across the structure. Loads were supported by tension in the upper portion of the bridge and compression in the lower parts. The result was a magnificent structure that spanned the width of the St. Lawrence River.

"Is this the new bridge?" asked Jolene.

"It depends on your definition of new," replied Dad. "It's much older than that one." He pointed at the Pierre Laporte suspension bridge beside them. This one was finished in 1917, but not without another incident."

"What kind of incident?" asked Michael. They were standing in a small park on the south side of the river, high on the cliffs, staring at the massive steel structure that linked life on this side of the St. Lawrence to life in Quebec City proper.

"After the collapse in 1907, a second bridge was begun in 1908. It was still a cantilever bridge but this time the design was slightly different. The bridge was much heavier and able to handle more load. And this time, the middle section was constructed independently and then floated down the river so that it could be raised into place using hydraulic jacks." Jolene imagined the central span of the bridge floating down the St. Lawrence, looking like a hollow upside-down ship. "Except as it was being hoisted into place, there was a loud cracking noise and the central span lurched sideways. The northern end held firm to the hangar, but the southern end tore away and the whole span plunged into the river."

"Was anybody hurt?" asked Stephan.

"Thirteen workers were killed," said Dad.

Jolene did the math. A total of eighty-eight men had been killed building this bridge.

"I've wanted to come here for years," said Dad. He raised his left hand and indicated the small silver ring that he always wore on his pinky finger. "This bridge is a symbol of why all Canadian engineers wear an iron ring."

"Really?" asked Jolene.

"The ring is a reminder to engineers that their decisions can impact the lives of citizens. Calculations must be checked and rechecked and safety margins are never to be compromised." He stared out at the steel diamonds high above the water. "When I graduated as an engineer, we had to attend a special iron ring ceremony and take an oath to maintain high ethical standards. I believe the original rings came from the wreckage of bridges, perhaps even this one." He paused. "When I was working as an engineer, I wore my ring on my other hand — the hand used for calculations and drawings. That's the tradition." He fell silent as cars sped above the water and Jolene wondered how many wreckages there had been because of human error.

"I'm going to get my camera equipment," Dad said, obviously anxious to recreate that wreckage in his museum.

Left on their own to explore, Jolene, Stephan, Michael and Grandpa wandered to the edge of the cliff overlooking the water. The St. Lawrence River was wide and peaceful in the sun. Tiny sequins of sunlight dotted the waves as Jolene tried to follow the river's curves and bends all the way to the Atlantic Ocean. Grandpa reminded them all that the St. Lawrence had a tide and Jolene watched now to see if the water was rising or falling. It was difficult to tell, but, she reasoned, since there was some muddy bank visible alongside the river's edge, the tide was probably part way in or out.

"The St. Lawrence has so much history," observed Grandpa. Stephan nodded but said nothing. He had been unusually quiet since they had arrived. "Is everything okay?" Grandpa asked him.

"It's fantastic," replied Stephan in a breathless whisper. "It's just . . . weird."

"Weird?"

Stephan's eyes darted the length of the bridge and then fell to the glittering water. "I feel as if they're here. The Mohawk men who died. It's as if they're all still here."

Grandpa smiled at him. "Places like this often have a powerful energy," he noted before moving along the cliffs with Michael.

Jolene watched the river. It shimmered with light and

sound and energy, but she could not feel the spirits of the Mohawk men. "Can you see them?" she asked Stephan, suddenly curious.

"No, but I can feel their spirits."

Jolene plucked a still-green blade of grass and held its smooth white root between her fingers. "Can they see you?"

"I don't know," said Stephan. "I don't think so." He turned his eyes to the sun and then levelled them on Jolene. "I envy you so much."

"Why?"

"It would be so awesome to be able to time-travel."

"I'm not so sure," said Jolene. "Your ancestors died."

"I know, but at least I'd be able to meet them." Stephan slowly scanned the area. "Is there a time crease here?"

"I haven't seen one, but probably."

Grandpa and Michael had moved to a nearby stand of bushes. Dad scampered across the top of the cliff, positioning his camera and changing lenses. "I need some pictures when the tide is completely out," he told them. "I'm going back to the RV to check the tide tables." Dad wiped his brow with the back of his hand. "Then I think we better get lunch."

The others followed leisurely, in no hurry to climb into a stifling hot vehicle. "Can we have pizza?" asked Michael. "It won't be as good as Gramps' pizza, but I still feel like it."

"It never is," said Jolene, smiling back at her grandfather. But he had not heard them; he was staring fixedly out towards the river. "Gramps?" called Jolene.

"Come on," urged Michael, taking in the situation. "I bet he's found a time crease." Michael loped back towards Grandpa with Jolene and Stephan on his heels.

"I thought people disappeared when they time-travelled," said Stephan to Jolene. "You certainly did."

"He's probably just looking through a window into the past," she replied. "Maybe you'll be able to see through it."

With quiet steps, Michael, Jolene and Stephan approached Grandpa, who seemed mesmerized. As they joined him, Jolene could feel a tingle as if a small current of electricity had run through her. The air trembled, revealing an unfinished lacework of girders stretched across the water. High above, steelmen in curly-brimmed hats, tweed vests and striped shirts moved with balanced precision and no safety harnesses. Men in boats ferried workers and equipment on the river. Jolene felt Stephan bump against her. "Can you see them?" she asked.

"Where?"

Michael pointed towards the construction site. Men scurried in and out of the bridge's shadow and a huge working platform of metal scaffolding on wheels sat on the bridge. "There!" he said, knocking Grandpa's hand and jolting him back into the present.

"Okay," said Grandpa, acknowledging their presence, "you can look, but you may not move."

Jolene felt Stephan shift, but she knew he couldn't see the window. He couldn't see the two men walking directly towards them in 1907. "The man with the hat seems to be in charge. He's probably the foreman," Grandpa told them. "Judging from their conversation, I'm guessing the younger one is an assistant engineer who worked with McClure."

Jolene leaned forward to hear what they were saying.

"I thought we were going to dismantle the traveller," said the younger man, pointing at the moveable platform of scaffolding near the edge of the bridge. "The men aren't comfortable with having the extra load on the structure. Not with those chords being bent and so far out of alignment. I told Mr. McClure so before he left."

Jolene guessed it must be close to the date of the bridge collapse, after the chords had been reported to be more than two inches out of alignment. Mr. McClure had probably gone to New York to see Theodore Cooper.

The foreman stopped and faced the young man. "I thought the same yesterday, but I'm not so inclined to think we need to be worried now."

"Why's that?"

"I had a dream last night that it was foolish to be nervous about bent girders. This here bridge has been designed by Mr. Theodore Cooper, one of the best engineers in the world. Why should we trouble ourselves over a few bends of steel?"

"I don't know," replied the other. "Can't you feel the men's fear?" Jolene's eyes swept upwards to where the men worked. Every so often, they stopped and looked around, but they continued to labour. "Mr. McClure himself went to New York this morning to see Mr. Cooper and meet with the Phoenix Bridge Company. It ain't normal, steel bending like this."

"Nonsense!" retorted the foreman. "I'm pulling that traveller out onto the bridge right now. May as well make the best of a beautiful afternoon."

He marched onto the iron walkways, climbing onto the moveable platform. Soon, it was moving out over the river. From great heights, eyes looked down. From far below, eyes looked up. Anxious eyes, thought Jolene. Fearful eyes. Proud eyes. Some of the men had boomed out from the Kahnawake reserve. Some of them would die soon. She shuddered.

Grandpa shifted and the window closed. Jolene turned towards Stephan who stood waiting in silent patience. "The men were worried," she said aloud. "Everyone was worried, except for the foreman."

Michael scoffed. "Because he had a dream that it would be okay." He set off towards the RV.

Jolene looked back at Stephan. Both the good dreams and the bad dreams were valuable he had told her. It was important to learn the right lessons from the bad ones. And perhaps they had. That was why engineers wore iron rings, a century later.

Grandpa twirled his moustache as he always did when he was thinking hard. Stephan's eyes shone with distant thoughts. Jolene turned away from both of them and headed towards the RV.

Chapter Thirteen

❦

LOW TIDE, DAD HAD discovered, was at suppertime, so they elected to spend the afternoon at the aquarium park, on the north side of the bridge. Jolene strolled off on her own, sitting in the empty stands above the harbour seal enclosure and watching the creatures splash, swim and suntan. Grandpa found her there, a fixture in the sunshine.

"Stephan and Michael are looking for you," he told her. "They're going to get ice-cream."

Ice-cream was a family tradition, but even it couldn't tempt Jolene to join the others. It was hard being around Stephan with so much time to think. He had been so kind, so attentive, and they had shared so much. How could she have misinterpreted those moments? She had told the girls how she felt about him. How could she have been so wrong? "I feel like some time alone," she told Grandpa.

"Okay," he said, patting her knee, "but Dad wants to head back to the south side soon — and the polar bears are awake."

The polar bears had been sleeping when she had visited the enclosure, but now Jolene gave in to Grandpa's persuasion and accompanied him to watch the creamy bears roll and play. From there, they joined the others at the entrance.

"We lost you," said Stephan. "Where were you?"

"Around," replied Jolene. They had left the RV parked on the south side of the Quebec Bridge, and now sauntered back over the river along the pedestrian and bicycle route. When they reached the middle, Michael peered over the rails of the bridge. "This would be an awesome place to play sticks, hey Jo?" he said, referring to a game they'd played as kids where they dropped sticks into the water on one side of a bridge and waited to see whose would emerge first on the other side.

A freighter was passing below them and the twins stayed to watch it. By the time they reached the south side, Dad was busy taking photos of the mud flats now visible below them. Grandpa's watch read quarter past five, the lowest tide of the day.

"Where's Stephan?" asked Michael.

"I don't know," said Grandpa.

"Maybe he's gone back to the RV," suggested Michael.

The recreational vehicle was parked a few hundred metres away, but Jolene knew it was still locked. Michael checked quickly and reported that Stephan wasn't there. Grandpa smoothed his moustache and Jolene fretted. It wasn't like Stephan to disappear without saying anything. A tiny drop of fear pooled inside her. Had he somehow discovered how to time-travel? Was he back in 1907 at this very minute?

She plucked a crimson leaf from a bush and went to find Grandpa. "I'm worried about Stephan, Gramps." Her grandfather looked up, and Jolene continued, "I know if he was able, he'd have gone back through the time crease. He desperately wanted to meet some of his First Nations ancestors."

Grandpa chewed the untrimmed hairs of his moustache. "He couldn't see the window into the past, could he?"

Jolene shook her head. It defied logic, but for some reason she sensed that Stephan was back in 1907. "No, but I think we should check and make sure he's not there."

Both Jolene and Michael were keen. Grandpa adjusted his suspenders and polished the face of his watch. He glanced over his shoulder where Dad was snapping photos.

"There's a trail down the hill," Dad called into the wind. "I'll be back shortly."

Jolene and Michael huddled closer to their grandfather. "I suppose we ought to make sure," Grandpa said finally.

Quickly, they slipped into the time crease, disappearing into the shadows of the bushes. Jolene felt the air grow warm, the pressure on her body and the feeling of being stretched like an elastic band. The darkness came, then suddenly gave way to daylight, 1907.

Grandpa and Michael had already arrived. The sound of steel on steel echoed in the river valley as the steelworkers laboured, their motions rhythmic and fluid. Michael scampered down the bank to the mud flats left behind by the receding tide and looked about for Stephan. Grandpa shaded his eyes and surveyed the bridge from atop the cliff. The crew had begun work on the central span, and dozens of men moved above the waters of the St. Lawrence. Staying halfway up the bank, Jolene called Stephan's name. She scanned the metal beams, her eyes zeroing in on one man after another. None of them resembled Stephan. He was almost the size of a man, but surely his modern clothing would make him stand out.

A steelworker called from high on the tower and Jolene watched the man, his body framed by a cloud. A stiff wind blew his words away, but she could see him gesturing at something in the sky and calling to one of the crew below him.

"I don't think Stephan's here, Jo," Grandpa called down to her.

The voice called again from the tower and Jolene squinted into the sun. Three of the men stood upright, having stopped working. A shrill cry filled the air and Jolene saw the bird immediately. A bald eagle, its massive wings spread, cruised on a gust of wind. It swooped and dived, passing close enough that the man on the tower could almost reach out and touch the eagle's long tail feathers. The men burst into exclamations, calling together in a language that Jolene did not recognize. "Those must be the Mohawk men," she said softly as the bird brushed past them a second time.

"Look at that eagle," called Michael, his arm raised.

Grandpa shaded his eyes. "I've never seen a bird of prey behave that way before."

Jolene would have to tell Stephan. For a split second, she hoped that he had been able to time-travel. That right now he was watching the bald eagle engage in this remarkable communication with the Kahnawake men on the bridge. It would have been Stephan's fourth encounter with an eagle. It would have meant that the bird was his animal spirit.

One of the men gripped a steel beam and leaned away from the bridge as if trying to reach something. Jolene strained to see. The eagle had dropped a tail feather and as it drifted closer, the man grabbed it with a joyous cry.

The shrill call of a whistle filled the air. A few of the men began climbing down off the bridge, while others on the mud flats dragged boats up past the tide line. Jolene scanned the riverbanks, looking for Stephan.

Michael scurried closer to the river, his runners squelching in the wet sandy soil. Two ducks quacked loudly, then turned tail and paddled into the water. Jolene ran towards the bridge. There was a lean figure on the platform of the cantilever that she thought she recognized. "Stephan," she cried. The worker did not hear her but there was something about the way he carried himself that sent adrenalin through Jolene's veins. "Stephan."

The worker turned. He had Stephan's build, with jet black hair and dark skin, but it was not Stephan. The shadow of the eagle fell across Jolene and the boy turned away. The bird shrieked and dived, passing close to her, then circling Michael and rocketing up the bank. Jolene climbed to higher ground as if the eagle had commanded her to do so. Michael clambered up beside her as Grandpa reached them. "The bridge is about to collapse," he told them. "It happened just before the last quitting whistle." They scrambled towards the higher ground where the time crease was situated. "I think we should go."

"Okay," said Jolene. But none of them moved. There was something as compelling as there was horrifying about a disaster.

On the mud flats below the bridge, a young man waved at the foreman inside the traveller. The moveable platform was well out near the centre of the bridge and the foreman who had dreamed of safety waved back. Jolene wanted to holler at them, but something held her back. She couldn't change history. She glanced up at the Kahnawake men walking high in the sky and swallowed the lump in her throat.

Above them the eagle shrieked, then flew towards the sun.

A resounding shot, like that of a cannon, sounded and

Jolene saw the bridge give way. Steel crashed, snapped, plunged and plummeted. The ground shook. The traveller lurched forward then flew through the air as the central span of the bridge crumbled. Jolene saw bodies airborne, steel beams crashing downwards. She heard the men cry and the thunderous splash as the central span of the bridge smashed into the river. The men disappeared beneath the water.

Within seconds, the southern arm of the cantilever crashed onto the mud banks with a loud fury. Broken beams of steel lay twisted and broken. Rigid metal lay crumpled in a mangled mess. In just fifteen seconds, the bridge had collapsed.

The boy she had mistaken for Stephan was gone. The man drawing up the boats on the flats was missing. The foreman and the traveller were nowhere in sight. Jolene saw a hand wave from beneath the metal girders on the river bank. A body floated to the surface in the middle of the river. The final quitting whistle sounded, echoing throughout the trembling valley.

"Let's go," screamed Michael, heading back down the hill. But Grandpa grabbed his shirt.

"We can't just leave them," protested Jolene.

Two men on the opposite shore had launched a boat. A few others followed. Heads bobbed to the surface of the St. Lawrence, arms flailed in the water and voices screamed for help.

"There's nothing we can do," said Grandpa.

"What do you mean?" asked Michael.

The men in the first boat had reached a survivor and hauled him aboard.

Grandpa put an arm around the shoulders of the twins. "Eleven men were rescued; all the others on the central span were pinned on the bottom of the river by steel beams. In just a few minutes, they'll drown."

Jolene squeezed her eyes shut. Her stomach flopped and goosebumps formed on her forearms.

Grandpa surveyed the chaos below them. "The worst part is," he said sadly, "this never should have happened."

Chapter Fourteen

STEPHAN WAS NOWHERE in sight when they passed through the time crease into the present. Jolene heard an eagle cry and looked up. It circled above a stand of trees near a residence farther along the cliff. Moments later Stephan burst from the trees and raced towards them.

"We saw the bridge collapse," said Michael in a sober voice before Stephan could speak. "There was nothing we could do." He turned and walked listlessly towards the RV. Grandpa hurried after him.

"It was terrible, Stephan," said Jolene.

"I know. I wanted you to leave."

Jolene looked up, her eyes puzzled.

"I was there, Jo."

"You went through the time crease?"

Stephan shook his head. "No. When you were all still on the bridge, I spotted an eagle circling this cliff. It led me to that stand of trees over there." He pointed at the high oaks behind them. "When I reached the trees, the eagle circled around and flew right towards me. It was so close and as it swept past me, it was like . . . like I went with it . . . into the past."

Jolene's jaw dropped. The eagle above the bridge. That eagle had been Stephan's eyes. That eagle had become Stephan's animal spirit. "You saw your ancestors, didn't you?"

"Yes," said Stephan in a measured voice. "One of them was high on the tower, wearing a wide-brimmed hat and a blue coat. When the bird swooped past him, he — "

"— Called to two others just below him."

"Yes," said Stephan.

"They stopped working and watched."

"And one of them reached out to catch a tail feather that the eagle dropped."

"That's right."

"Then the eagle saw you and Michael."

"And chased us up the cliff towards the time crease."

Again, Stephan nodded. "Before it could leave, there was this loud metallic crash and the bridge crumpled." He grimaced and she wondered what it must have looked like from above. "The Kahnawake men were killed."

Jolene wrung her hands together. "I'm sorry."

"It's okay," said Stephan. "They're still here."

They stood in silence, the sun on their backs, lost in their own thoughts. Thoughts of the past, thoughts of the present, thoughts of life, death and struggle. Thoughts of hope and hopelessness. Jolene relinquished her thoughts to the wind. There were no answers. Only thin iron rings worn on working hands that might prevent this from happening again.

The wind carried Dad's voice to them, rousing them both from their reverie. "I've got the most incredible photos," he called out. "Too bad they're not from 1907, but then we can't time-travel, can we?"

Neither Jolene nor Stephan replied.

A half-moon of sun rested on the horizon as Jolene reached the octagonal gazebo overlooking the St. Lawrence and settled on a wooden bench. After a solemn night, they had spent a day visiting the National Assembly and museum exhibits, following the stone walls that had once fortified the old settlement of Quebec, passing through the revolving bronze doors of the Chateau Frontenac and exploring the boutiques and art galleries that lined the narrow cobblestone streets. Lunch had been *tourtière* and pea soup at a tiny bistro, and dessert had been taffy on a stick — warm maple syrup poured into an ice trough and then hardened around a flat wooden popsicle stick. As the sun slid towards the river, they had climbed the smooth, wooden stairs of the governor's promenade and followed the plank sidewalks along the high cliffs above the river. The gazebo marked the end of the promenade, on the edge of the Plains of Abraham where Montcalm and Wolfe had once staged their historic battle.

Jolene was weary of walking but, she sensed, her fatigue was more emotional than physical. For the past two days, she had done her best to keep her emotions hidden from Stephan. All day she had made a conscious effort not to watch him as he ambled and explored, not to lean towards his voice when he spoke, not to smile up at him as he perused the goods in the shops over her shoulder.

"Hey sis," said Michael, joining her in the gazebo and slinging an arm around her shoulders. "Everything all right?"

"Sure, why?"

"'Cause I know you." Michael grinned at her. "Why don't you just talk to him?"

Jolene blinked in surprise. "Who?" she demanded.

Michael rolled his eyes. "Montcalm," he said sarcastically. "They went that way." He pointed away from the river before dashing out of the gazebo.

Jolene watched him go, hoping that she had deceived Stephan more successfully than her twin brother. The effort had left her drained and hollow, and she was glad that she now found herself alone. Her eyes followed the route of the river, a dark ribbon in the twilight, back to the silhouette of the Quebec Bridge. Just yesterday, she had been frantic with worry that Stephan would be hurt or killed in the 1907 collapse. Her fear had been real, her concern genuine, her emotions intense and strong. There was no denying that — or her feelings for him. Her head ached with confusion. How, she wondered, did you just stop caring about someone? How did you just make the feelings go away?

"It's beautiful, isn't it?"

Stephan's voice came from behind her, but she did not turn to look at him. Instead, she took a deep breath and resolved to continue her brave façade. He said nothing more, but joined her on the bench and gazed out towards the river. It should have been a tranquil moment, but his eyes were clearly troubled. "Michael said I'd find you here."

"He did?"

"Have I done something wrong, Jo?" Stephan asked suddenly.

"No. Why?" Jolene replied quickly, too quickly, she thought.

"I just have this feeling that you've been avoiding me."

"No, not at all." Her voice was shrill and false. He made no response. "I'm sorry," she confessed after a moment. "I'm just tired." Additional words eluded her.

"I was thinking about the last few days," Stephan began slowly. "It's been awesome having you here, really awesome for me."

The blazing red of the sun had diffused to an intense coral wash in the sky. Jolene squirmed in her seat. Her friendship, she knew, meant a lot to him. And he had been a good friend — kind, helpful and honest. It was more than she had been these past few days. "Stephan," she said, "I owe you an apology." She looked up into his eyes. "It's just that I feel like I've made such a fool of myself. If you'd told me earlier about Sarah, I wouldn't have been such an idiot."

Confusion clouded Stephan's eyes momentarily and then he burst into laughter. To Jolene's surprise, he clasped her hands in his. "You little fool," he said affectionately.

"What!" stammered Jolene. "You told me . . ."

"That it was hard when a girl liked you and you didn't like her, especially when you liked someone else," repeated Stephan. Jolene nodded. "I was talking about Sarah and you," he told her grinning, "not you and Sarah."

As Jolene's brain performed mental gymnastics, Stephan leaned towards her. "Here," he said, "maybe this will help sort things out." He kissed her, and suddenly Jolene understood. It had been Sarah who had showered him with unwanted affection. It had been Sarah whom he had gently informed he didn't share her feelings, while all the time wanting to be with Jolene. She slid towards him and his arms encircled her. Embarrassment and relief gave way to joy as the sun crashed into the river.

For as long as they dared, Jolene and Stephan sat together in the warmth of the evening then reluctantly went to join the others, walking hand in hand until voices parted their fingers. The last rays of sun had vanished and so had any doubts she might have had, leaving behind a feeling of incredible, shared happiness.

Grandma Rose's house was teeming with life when the RV pulled onto her street the next afternoon. Stephan's parents, who had arrived home from Brazil, burst out the front door, embraced Stephan and greeted Dad, Grandpa and the twins. After promising to return shortly for supper, they disappeared next door. "See you soon," Stephan called over his shoulder.

"Soon," replied Jolene, but Mom was already pulling her inside and upstairs.

"Come and see," she urged as Jolene scooped Chaos off the bottom stair and transported him upstairs. Grandma Rose was also herding her up the staircase, instructing Michael to hurry up and join them.

On the desk in the green bedroom sat a new computer. "A computer!" exclaimed Jolene. "I thought —"

"Nonsense," interrupted Grandma Rose, sliding into the desk chair. After a quick adjustment to her glasses, she proudly clicked on the internet icon.

"You're on the internet?" asked Michael.

"We got the hook-up yesterday," said Mom. "Watch this!"

The twins watched incredulously as their grandmother typed in a URL address and the Antikythera mechanism quilt appeared alongside a photo of Grandma Rose. "Rose's Quilts," read Jolene aloud. "Custom order or choose from a large selection of featured patterns."

"You have a website!" exclaimed Michael, stating the obvious.

"And an order," said Grandma proudly. "Although it came from a neighbour, not the website."

"It's only been up for an hour and a half," said Mom, laughing.

"That's great!" Jolene was busy stitching the pieces together. Quilting was what Grandma Rose loved to do most, and money was a concern. Her grandmother was scrolling through the website and Jolene noticed that almost all the quilts she had made were featured. Jolene beamed at her mother. It was a great idea — a chance for her grandmother to earn money at home, doing what she loved best. "What's a custom-made quilt worth?" she asked.

"It depends on the size and the work, but they can easily sell for a couple of thousand dollars or more," advised Mom.

"Wow!" said Michael. "Wanna teach me to quilt, Gram?"

"I think that ought to be a project for Christmas," said Grandma Rose, "when I come out and visit you in Calgary."

"You're coming for Christmas?" Was there no end of surprises, thought Jolene.

"By train," explained Grandma Rose, "so I don't have to fly."

"The passenger train goes to Edmonton," added Mom, "but it's only a short drive to pick her up. It's no big deal if she stays for a month or so."

A month? Jolene tried to hide her shock. In past years, the prospect of Grandma and Mom spending more than a week together had been impossible to fathom.

"There's really nothing to keep me here. And once the attic is rented out, the house will be taken care of and I'll be free to travel — with my quilting projects."

"Any other surprises?" asked Michael. "Or are you just about done?"

"Just that Mrs. Walter's niece is interested in buying Grandma's car," said Mom proudly. "She's going to rent the attic suite. That way she can be close to family and still have her independence. Before we go, we have to move all the boxes out of the attic, throw out a bunch of junk, and have a plumber and electrician check things out."

Jolene was suddenly envious. How she would have loved to have the attic beside Stephan's, but then he wouldn't be there forever either. She watched her mom with unhidden admiration. In just three days, she had unearthed two new sources of income for Grandma Rose, given her a sense of pride and purpose, and enabled her to come visit them. That would take the pressure off her parents to spend all their vacations in Montreal, and already she looked guilt-free. Guilt-free and content. Not only that, Grandma Rose was just as happy.

"So does this mean I can check my e-mail?" asked Jolene.

"Sure," said Grandma, pushing herself away from the desk. The chair went spinning, sending her lurching forward. The twins burst into laughter.

Jolene handed the kitten to her brother and waited for everybody to clear out of her bedroom. As soon as the room was free, she signed on to her e-mail. She opened the last message from Ellie and read it. *If he tries to kiss me during the last dance, should I let him?* Tapping the reply button, Jolene responded with a single word. *Absolutely!* She would write a longer message later when they had moved on from Montreal. Right now, she had precious time to spend with Stephan and her family.

"So," said Mom, when the final piece of chocolate cake had been consumed after the evening meal, "what are the plans for tomorrow?" She looked around the table where the two neighbouring families had assembled for dinner.

"Tom has to teach," said Stephan's mother, Mirette, "but I'm free to go shopping in the afternoon." She looked imploringly at Mom, and Jolene had a sudden vision of the two of them as teenagers, their purses slung over their shoulders in the mall. "Want to come, Jolene?"

Jolene dabbed at a chocolate crumb. "Actually, I want to go to the Archives. I'm trying to finish the family tree before we leave."

"We e-mailed a request for some certificates," explained

Stephan, not bothering to mention who they were for. "They'll be available for pickup tomorrow."

"Okay," said Dad. "Michael?"

"No special plans," said Michael. "Maybe I'll tag along with Jo and Stephan." His eyes shone with mischief and he waited until his sister scowled at him. "Or maybe I won't."

"Actually," said Mom, "I think you'd better get a haircut. You're looking like a sheepdog." She glanced at Dad. "Can you take Michael, Doug?"

"Sure," agreed Dad, running a hand through his thinning hair. "I'll get a cut at the same time."

Beneath the table, Stephan's hand found Jolene's and squeezed it tightly.

The sky was spitting at them, but neither Jolene nor Stephan noticed. Stephan's arm was around her waist and hers around his. Given their height difference, Jolene suspected that he was making as much an effort to shorten his strides as she was to lengthen hers. But it was no effort to carry on a conversation and they never seemed to run out of things to say to one another.

By the time they had reached the Archives, Jolene didn't think her happiness coefficient could go any higher. The clouds had cleared and a brilliant blue sky stretched above them. "I'm guessing that the certificate will confirm that Poppy died in the fire," Stephan said gently as they approached the desk.

"I know," said Jolene, although she had to admit that a small piece of her still harboured the hope that they would find that Poppy and Suzanna had lived.

They had almost reached the front of the document pick-up queue, and Stephan motioned for her to go ahead. A young woman with manicured eyebrows handed them an envelope, and they retreated to a quiet bench. Carefully, Jolene opened it to reveal a photocopied death certificate. It told her everything she had thought it would. The death of Poppy Dumont had occurred on January 9, 1927, and the cause of death was listed as smoke inhalation. An almost identical certificate existed for Suzanna. It was a sad ending to what should have been a happy story.

Jolene slid her hand into the envelope a second time and withdrew Suzanna's birth certificate. "Suzanna Giselle Dumont," she read aloud, "born May 12, 1915, at 3: 54 a.m to Annalise (Smith) Dumont and Pierre Dumont."

The last certificate was Poppy's birth certificate. "Poppy Elizabeth Dumont," read Jolene. Although the birth date was the same, the time was listed as 7:59 p.m. "That's a long time to be in labour," she remarked.

"Look!" Stephan's fingers pointed at the names of the parents and Jolene felt the blood stop in her veins.

In the space for the mother's name was written *Nora Richardson*. The father's name was listed as *Marc Dumont*. "That's my great-grandmother," said Jolene, breathless, recalling the picture of the beautiful young bride. "And Marc

Dumont is Suzanna's dad's brother. When I was at Poppy and Suzanna's, I saw a photo of him on the wall. He was killed in the war and the girls called him their uncle."

Stephan looked confused. "I thought Nora was married to Claude — "

"Renaud," finished Jolene. She had recorded his name on her family tree next to Nora's. "But they were married in 1920, and Poppy was born in 1915."

"Which means," said Stephan, "that the girls weren't actually twins."

"There fathers were brothers," reasoned Jolene, "so they must have been cousins. That explains their family resemblance at least."

"So," continued Stephan, "your great-grandmother, Nora, married Marc Dumont — "

"I don't think so," said Jolene, pointing at Nora's name. No married name was listed on the certificate. "But she had a child with him." Her mind raced. "Then Marc died in World War I and for some reason, Nora decided to leave her child with Marc's brother and his wife, and pretend the girls were twins."

"Maybe it had something to do with her being an unwed mother," said Stephan.

"Maybe," said Jolene, her mind slotting information into place. "But what I don't understand is why Grandma Rose didn't mention that she had a half-sister."

"I'm guessing she didn't know," said Stephan. "It might

have been easier for Nora to give Poppy up completely and pretend she didn't have a daughter."

"But why would she do that? Wouldn't that just break a mother's heart?"

Stephan shrugged as Jolene tried hard to visualize her family tree. "Grandma Rose was born on January 11th, 1927," she said, recalling the date she had written, "two days after the fire at the Laurier Palace Theatre that killed Poppy." Her eyes shone as a crucial piece of puzzle fell into place. "That must have been what the phone call was about. That was the shock that triggered Grandma Rose's birth." Jolene was anxious to tell her grandmother. Perhaps it would relieve her guilt about Nora's death.

Jolene stuck her hand in the empty envelope. "I wish we'd thought to inquire about Danielle," she said, sliding the documents back inside.

"I thought Danielle survived."

"I think she did," said Jolene. "I'd just like to know."

"I see your point," said Stephan. "Hang on a second." He left Jolene seated on the bench and approached the information desk. When he returned, he was smiling excitedly. "Come on," he said. "Let's go."

"Where to?" asked Jolene.

"La Grande Bibliothèque, to see the old newspapers."

"Do you think they'll list the victims?" asked Jolene hopefully. "There were so many of them."

Jolene watched the librarian thread the microform reel onto the machine and turn it clockwise on the take-up reel. "The newspapers are chronological," she explained. "Use these arrow buttons to move forwards and backwards, the focus button to adjust the clarity, and the zoom to move in and out." She smiled at them. "And call if you need help."

Newsprint flickered across the screen until the date January 10, 1927, appeared. Except for the headline, which read *76 Killed in East End Theatre Fire Panic*, the old print of the articles was small and difficult to decipher. A photo of firefighters outside the theatre was featured on the front page. Jolene read the caption, the familiar scene evoking fresh pain. The names of the dead were not included. A day later, the newspaper showed pictures of the funeral procession with the headline *Impressive Funeral of Theatre Victims: 100,000 Bow in Sorrow as Cortege of Hearses Passes through Streets*. Beside the pictures of the hearses, were smaller photos of the victims. "I met her," said Jolene, as a picture of one of the girls she'd drunk milkshakes with came into view. There were no pictures of Poppy or Suzanna, but their names appeared in the list of the dead. Jolene skimmed the rest of the victims' names. There wasn't a single Danielle listed among them. "Well, at least I didn't change history," she said, relieved.

Stephan was still staring at the screen and Jolene followed his gaze to an article that related the tragic story of a local constable who had entered the cinema during the fire only to discover all three of his children amongst those who had succumbed to death in the stairwell. Another told of a man who had gone to work, leaving behind his children, only to return home to find them all missing after they had disobeyed his orders not to attend the showing of the film.

"It's such a pity," muttered Stephan. "If the audience hadn't panicked, they would probably all have gotten out without a single injury."

Jolene skimmed the newsprint. The city would be holding an inquiry into the tragedy. Curious, she pressed the forward button, flickering through newspapers until she found an article on the results of the investigation. "Look," said Stephan, pointing at the screen, "the building wasn't built to the proper regulations."

"And it was overcrowded," added Jolene.

"But they never did determine definitively the cause of the fire," said Stephan. "They suspect it was ashes smouldering beneath the floorboards or maybe faulty wiring."

"All I know for sure," said Jolene, "is that Danielle's father will never let her go to another film."

"Need any help?" asked the librarian, stopping by the table.

"No thanks," said Jolene. "I think we found what we were looking for."

The librarian's eyes flickered over the screen. "The Laurier Palace Theatre fire," she said knowingly. "That fire changed the law in Quebec for many years."

"It did?"

"After that tragedy, the Catholic Church campaigned hard to keep children out of the theatres. They won and Quebec passed a law prohibiting kids under the age of sixteen from attending movies and plays. It lasted until 1967."

"Wow!" said Jolene as the librarian moved on to help someone else. She turned to Stephan. "Everything that happens has repercussions, doesn't it?"

"And most we never know."

Jolene looked around the library. Drawers of microforms containing old newspapers filled one wall. "There might be papers from 1907," she suggested.

But Stephan shook his head. "I think I've had enough for one day."

Jolene, too, had had her fill of tragedy and death. They returned the microform, thanked the librarian and left the library. But it was difficult to resume the easy chatter they had shared earlier. Seeing the newspaper articles had made the fire all too real again, and Jolene found herself contemplating how a single event could affect so many lives. It had touched her grandmother's as well as her own, just as the bridge collapse had touched Stephan's life. But, she thought, squeezing Stephan's hand, at least something wonderful had come out of the disasters. She and Stephan had found members of their families, and each other. She had a sudden urge to celebrate.

A sign on the other side of the street caught her attention

and she broke into a run, pulling Stephan along with her. "There's something I want to do," she replied in response to his questioning glance.

Twenty minutes later, they were posed in front of the camera. "Okay," said the photographer at the Old Fashioned Portraits Studio kiosk. "Are you ready?"

Jolene looked up at Stephan who looked handsome and regal in his First Nations costume. She glanced down at her own dress from the twenties and adjusted her cloche hat. "Ready," she said.

"All right," said the photographer. He hesitated. "You don't really go together, you know."

Jolene looked up at Stephan who was grinning at her. "Yes, we do," she said, as the camera flashed.

Chapter Fifteen

"HEY, GRAM," CALLED Jolene as they entered the house. Her grandmother was in the kitchen, on the phone, a magnifying glass resting on the yellow pages. "Is there any chance that you ever had a half sister?"

Grandma Rose looked up, a bewildered expression on her face. "Nobody ever mentioned one." She pushed her glasses down on the bridge of her nose. "Why?" she asked, her ear to the phone.

Jolene started to respond, but Grandma Rose held up one finger, then held the phone away from her to push a button. She must have reached an automated reply system.

Jolene traipsed into the living room with Stephan, but

her grandmother hollered after her. "I found that shoebox I was telling you about up in the attic. It's on the dining room table." Jolene heard her grandmother speak into the phone. "Hello. Is this Canyon Plumbing?"

"Want to take it out on the porch?" asked Stephan as Jolene picked up the dusty box.

Sitting side by side on the swing, Jolene peered inside. The first framed picture was of her great-grandmother, Nora, and her great-grandfather, Claude, on their wedding day. It was slightly less posed and static than the one she'd seen earlier. Jolene was still studying it when Stephan let out a gasp. Reaching into the box, he withdrew a framed picture of Poppy.

"Look at that!" exclaimed Jolene.

"Your double." Stephan sighed. "At least she wasn't your omen of death. I was so worried she would be." Jolene felt the colour drain from her face. Until that moment, she had never considered the possibility that Poppy's presence might have signalled her own death. Obviously Stephan had.

She leaned against him as he turned his attention back to the shoebox. There was another photograph, a picture of a young couple, obviously in love. On the back, someone had scrawled *Pierre and Annalise, August 1914*. She stared at the photo of Suzanna's parents. Annalise might have been expecting her daughter when this photo was taken. Who could have imagined how their lives would unravel then?

Beneath that photo was another one, a dog-eared black

and white picture of six women in dancing costumes. An arrow pointed to the woman on the far right and a notation read *Annalise.*

Jolene studied the tall, long-legged beauty. She wore a short, layered skirt, a bodice with a heart shaped neckline, and an enticing, reckless smile. The other women were dressed identically. "Poppy and Suzanna told me their mother was a vaudeville dancer before she married," she told Stephan. "That must have been a crazy life."

The final piece of paper had been fastidiously folded. Jolene opened it to reveal a playbill, a poster advertising a double matinée featuring two films, *Upstage* and *The Devil's Gulch.* An insert of a beautiful brunette actress with compelling eyes and a whimsical smile caught her eye. *Starring Norma Shearer* read the playbill.

Jolene regarded the documents thoughtfully. They belonged to her great-grandmother's other life, the one that, she guessed, Grandma Rose and her family had known nothing about.

Stephan's head was bent low over two photos in his hand, the ones of the dancing women and the wedding photo. "Look at this woman," he said, pointing to the dancer beside Annalise. "Isn't that Nora?"

Jolene scrutinized the picture. It was definitely Nora, dressed as a vaudeville dancer. And that definitely fit the puzzle. "Annalise and Nora danced together," she said quietly, "and might have been sister-in-laws if Marc hadn't died in the war."

"Probably," said Stephan. "That certainly explains why Nora would have trusted Annalise and Marc with her daughter."

Jolene picked up the photo of Poppy and polished the glass. "I wonder if Poppy knew that she wasn't really Suzanna's twin?" she asked aloud. "Somehow, I doubt it." Would Annalise and Pierre have told her one day? Had Poppy even met her real mother? "I remember," said Jolene, slowly voicing a thought that had just occurred to her, "that the girls told me about their mother's friend who was an awesome dancer. She visited them every year, and they called her aunty."

"You think it was Nora?"

"I think so." But so many questions remained. Why had Nora married Claude and moved away to the farm? Why had she told none of her children of Poppy's existence? What motivation had she had for leaving her daughter with Pierre and Annalise and failing to tell Poppy she was her mother? There were some family mysteries that she suspected would always remain mysteries.

Grandma Rose peered over Jolene's shoulder. It had taken most of the evening to explain the family connections and what had happened to Poppy. Jolene had turned all the official documents over to Grandma Rose and identified all the people she could in her great-grandmother Nora's pictures. Now it was time to officially add Poppy to the family tree. Beside the box containing Nora Richardson's name, Jolene had added another one bearing the name *Marc Dumont*. A double line joined the two boxes indicating a union of a couple. Beneath that double line, Jolene added another box with the name of their daughter, *Poppy Elizabeth Dumont*, along with her birth date. Grandma Rose's name, as well as those of her brothers, Gus and Edward, appeared on the same horizontal line beneath the double lines uniting Nora and Claude Renaud.

"I always wanted a sister," said Grandma Rose. "Did you notice that my mother named us both after flowers?"

Jolene hadn't, but she smiled at Grandma Rose's observation. Poppy's picture stood next to Jolene's and Michael's school pictures on the end table in the living room. All evening long, various members of the family had studied them, marvelling at the girls' resemblance.

Mom, who had been watching and listening with a smile all evening, looked at her watch and chased the twins upstairs to bed. She joined Jolene a few minutes later. "Grandma Rose was pretty excited. Family's pretty important to her."

"Speaking of which," said Jolene, "what happened with you and Grandma while we were away in Quebec City? It was a pretty amazing transformation."

"Yes," agreed Mom, "and a long over-due one." She sighed. "I'm not sure why misunderstandings always occur with the truly special people in your life, but they do." She paused. "I guess it's because you leave yourself vulnerable when you care, especially if they don't feel the same way as you do." She stroked Jolene's hair. "I don't suppose you understand that yet."

"I understand better than you think."

"It's ironic, but true," said Mom, reaching down to scratch Chaos' ears. The kitten was cuddled against Jolene's feet. "You only hurt the ones you care about. The rest don't care enough to be hurt."

"But," said Jolene, "as long as you keep caring, anything is possible." Her mother switched off the lamp on the night table, sending the dream catcher spinning gracefully in the darkness.

About the Author

Cathy Beveridge enjoys researching and writing about historical Canadian disasters, believing that these stories offer insight into our country and human nature, in general. While researching her other disaster novels, *Shadows of Disaster*, *Chaos in Halifax* and *Stormstruck*, Cathy discovered two other tragic events from Canada's past. The Laurier Palace Theatre fire (1927) of Montreal and the Quebec Bridge collapse (1907) left her troubled by the knowledge that both these disasters could have and should have been prevented, a fact that inspired her to write *Tragic Links*. Cathy's novels have won the Snow Willow Award and have been nominated for the Rocky Mountain Book Award, the Diamond Willow Award and the Red Cedar Award. Other publications include two contemporary young-adult novels published by Thistledown Press, *Offside* and *One on One*. Some of Cathy's short stories can be found in anthologies such as *Beginnings: Stories of Canada's Past* (Ronsdale Press, 2001) and *Up all Night* (Thistledown Press, 2001). Cathy resides in Calgary with her husband, three daughters, a dog and a cat. She works as an author and writing consultant, conducting writing workshops with students and providing professional development seminars on creative writing.

Marquis Book Printing Inc.

Québec, Canada
2009